LOST ADVENTURE RESCUED
FROM OBSCURITY

The Red Spider, written in April 1948, was lost until 1975 when records were found of what appeared to be a hitherto unknown Doc Savage novel.

Finally in 1978 the only surviving copy of the manuscript was located among Kenneth Robeson's papers.

THE ULTIMATE
DOC SAVAGE® ADVENTURE

The Red Spider stands as a high-water mark in the series.

Bantam Books by Kenneth Robeson
Ask your bookseller for the books you have missed

THE RED SPIDER

A Doc Savage® Adventure

KENNETH ROBESON

Afterword by Will Murray

THE RED SPIDER

*A Bantam Book / published by arrangement with
The Condé Nast Publications, Inc.*

PRINTING HISTORY
Bantam edition / July 1979

ISBN 0-553-12787-X

Published simultaneously in the United States and Canada

*Bantam Books are published by Bantam Books, Inc. Its trade-
mark, consisting of the words "Bantam Books" and the portrayal of a bantam, is Registered in U.S. Patent and Trademark
Office and in other countries. Marca Registrada. Bantam
Books, Inc., 666 Fifth Avenue, New York, New York 10019.*

PRINTED IN THE UNITED STATES OF AMERICA

1

At fifteen minutes past six a Colonel Renwick reached a village named Tyrolstadt, in the American zone. Lunging out of the staff car, he glanced at his wristwatch for the time—it was eighteen-fifteen the way he read it—and he blurted, "Holy cow!" He began to run.

The ramp had been built on the *familen abfahrt*, an easy ski trail at the east edge of the village, and the Colonel reached the spot red-faced and panting. A radar technician named Roberts grinned at the Colonel and said, "Made it!"

"Yeah," gasped Colonel Renwick. "I had a flat tire this side of Salzburg. After that, I had visions of the top brass snatching these chickens off my shoulders."

"There's more than your chickens at stake."

"That's right too."

"Well, you got here," said Roberts. "Eighteen-forty is Z hour."

The early darkness had a lacing of moonlight, and there was no snow here in the valley, but enough snow smeared the adjacent mountains to make them look like great soiled goats. The ramp was not a terrific thing as rocket-launching ramps came, but it was impressive standing there alone in the alien mountain beauty, like a river bridge out of its element, somewhat. About thirty men were around, either looking or working, more in uniform than not.

"The Russians pushed their hard noses into it, I see," remarked the Colonel.

"Yes. Half a dozen of them," said Roberts.

"Are they full of bliss?"

"Ignorance being bliss, you mean?"

"Exactly."

"I believe they're bliss up to here," said Roberts.

"I hope they stay that way."

Roberts said warningly, "Let's change the subject. No telling where you run into a lip-reader these days." He pointed and added, "They're getting ready to ramp the rocket now."

The service party whipped the tarpaulin off the cart on which the rocket was resting, and a loading crane arched up with gears whining. Floodlights came on and covered the scene with an unnecessary amount of blinding light. The radar-tracker keyman in Position Zero jumped out of his nest of apparatus and cursed the floodlight operators for a bunch of Kentucky baboons. They ignored him. The loaders began cursing; the Russians had rushed in and started taking pictures and measurements.

The Russian move was obviously planned, concerted, and surely intended to be as much obstructionist and irritating as fact-getting. As anyone knew, photographs of the outside of the rocket and the tape-measurements they insisted on taking wouldn't tell anybody much about the complicated guts of the thing. The Ivans went right ahead. Camera flashbulbs popped. Steel-tape rulers and notebooks waved. Russians shoved Yankees, and the favor was returned. Colonel Renwick waved his arms and screamed for order. He had a considerable voice, the Colonel had; peasant dogs began barking in alarm as far as two miles away.

With some order restored, Colonel Renwick made them a little speech in which he said he was clarifying the situation.

Radar, the Colonel said, wasn't a new thing, so he wouldn't bother to tell anybody what it was. He presumed everyone knew it was a process of bouncing very short radio waves off an object and catching the reflections and showing them on a screen similar to that in a television tube.

Jamming a radar set so it wouldn't function reliably, the Colonel said, was not a new endeavor either. It had been done with varying success with several methods, beginning with releasing numerous ribbons of metalized paper in the sky, during the last war.

But a method of really messing up the atmosphere over a considerable area so that radar was really jammed, continued the Colonel, was another matter. It was theoretically possible, though, if one ionized the atmospheric layers, preferably those below the tropospheric zone, so that radar microwave lengths were refracted the same way that shortwave radio frequencies are affected by the ionization mystery of the Heaviside layer.

This was the purpose of the experiment tonight. Thanks to the electronic genius of Thomas J. "Long Tom" Roberts, eminent New York electrical engineer in his own right, and associate of the supereminent scientist and adventurer Doc Savage, they were going to show that Yankee ingenuity had triumphed again, and warm-minded nations might as well discard their radar for all the good

3

it would do them. There was a slight implication here that the Russians weren't too far from the Colonel's mind.

The eminent Long Tom Roberts listened to the oration, mentally noting a few flaws in it. Except that the mention of Doc Savage wasn't exaggerated —in Long Tom's opinion, it was hard to exaggerate Doc Savage—the speech was a bunch of mush. The facts that were there were all true, so it wasn't mush because of that. It just happened that the Russians were understood to have a radar-jamming rocket similar to the one being shot off tonight. It also happened that the Americans had a considerably better one under wraps. The omissions, rather than the insertions, flawed the Colonel's oratory.

The rocket was to go north to the North Sea.

It didn't. It climbed to twenty thousand feet, threw a whing-ding, and headed for Moscow.

This, as far as the Americans were concerned, seemed to be a calamity. The radar-check network was excellent; the course of the rocket was graphed, charted, and annotated straight to the Iron Curtain. Presumably it passed through and beyond Moscow somewhere and struck the earth or disintegrated in midair when its push-charge was exhausted, depending on whether or not the self-demolition head worked.

The American ambassador sent a note of apology to Moscow. The American commanding general in the zone sent Moscow a note demanding return of the rocket remnants uninspected. The Russians ignored both notes. A writer for Izvestia called the Americans imperialistic toads, boors, thieves, bloated monkeys, said that two thousand people

starved to death in New York City that day, and
Florida had declared war on California. Molotov
vetoed.

In the privacy of the staff car, Colonel Renwick
and Long Tom Roberts shook hands ceremoniously.

"I would say," remarked the Colonel, "that we
suckered them."

"A perfect scald at this end," Long Tom Roberts
agreed. "Or it looked like it, anyway."

"You sure they won't be able to spot an aircraft
following the path that rocket took?"

"For about three hours," said Roberts, "Ivan's
radar will be blind as a bat."

"How was the timing?"

"On the nose."

"Then the rest is up to Doc."

"The rest," said Long Tom Roberts, suddenly
sober, "is really going to be something."

Colonel Renwick looked at him thoughtfully.
"You like excitement. Don't you kind of hate missing it?"

Roberts shuddered. "I don't like it when it's
tied up with sudden death the way this is going
to be."

2

The pilot's voice had a faraway, cut-in-glass quality in the ear-plug receivers. He said, "Altitude thirty-four thousand, two hundred and fifteen seconds from Check Nine. Airspeed Mach one-point-sixteen. All green."

Doc Savage said, "All green. Right. All green here, too."

It was already hot in the ship. At slightly under a speed of one thousand miles per hour, there was considerable friction-generated heat, and the refrigeration mechanism was performing as usual —which meant that it either kept things too hot or too cold.

Doc Savage was not riding in the most advantageous spot, either. He was in the pop-off blister, and they needed to do some more design work on it, because the streamlining which had looked well enough in the wind tunnels was not perfect at this speed. Or perhaps it was the altitude; thirty-four thousand feet was pretty close to the earth for speed over sound. The trouble, though, was that if they went higher, above fifty thousand, where the conditions were better, there was a chance the Soviet radar might top the blackout path made by the runaway rocket—the runaway so carefully computed—and so they were keeping

7

at a comparatively low level. The speed was being kept down, not much over breakthrough, but it was still uncomfortably hot.

Doc Savage waited without much visible suspense on his rather pleasant bronze face. The moonlight that came in through the transparent stress plastic of the blister had a bluish quality that added to the metallic impression that his face gave, and enhanced the slightly darker bronze of his hair, and the remarkable flake-gold aspect of his eyes, which were probably his most striking characteristic.

He wasn't particularly comfortable in the pop-off blister. Each time he tried to shift position to let a little circulation move to another part of his body, he was reminded that the space had been made for a man of average size. He didn't qualify as average. This was not the first time that it had not been an asset to be, as a newspaper had called it, a muscular marvel.

"Cloud floor?" Doc asked, laying a fingertip against the throat microphone.

"Cloud floor twenty-one thousand below," the pilot responded instantly. "Position now forty seconds past. Check Ten. Airspeed Mach one-point-fourteen. Reducing."

"Thanks."

"Heat bothering you, sir?" asked the pilot.

"Not much. I'm wringing wet, is all."

There was a moment of silence. The silence, considering everything, was really remarkable, because at that speed they were flouting sound. The silence of beyond-sound flight, Doc Savage reflected, was one thing that he would probably never become quite accustomed to; it was too much of a contrast to the thousands of hours he had flown before jet was developed.

He heard the pilot's voice saying, "I hope it doesn't give you cold, sir. There will be what you might call quite a draft when you take to the parachute. And drafts are hell for colds."

In a moment the pilot added, "What are you laughing at, sir."

"The idea of thinking about catching cold in a situation like this just struck me as funny," Doc told him. "Sorry. No offense. Where are we?"

"Position eight seconds past Check Eleven—two hundred and fourteen miles from Moscow. Altitude still thirty-four thousand feet."

"Break through at Check Twelve."

"I understand, sir."

The pilot's voice had a sudden high edge of tension in it. He was experienced with rocket ships, so going through the wild and still unpredictable zone of compressibility surrounding the speed of sound was not new to him; but doing it had evidently given him nothing but respect. The low altitude wasn't any asset, either.

"Deceleration."

"Right," Doc said.

"Barrel four off."

"Okay here."

"Speed now Mach one-point-zero-nine. Cutting Barrel three."

"All green."

There was no sign that the ship was losing speed; she was pinned in that weird silence, and only if one looked down and saw that the clouds were seemingly moving, was there much impression of existence at all.

9

"Time zero minus fourteen. Error minus two. Airspeed Mach one-zero-zero-two—I mean, one-point,zero-two." The pilot sounded flustered. "Hell, we're going through, sir. Cross your fingers and pray," he added.

Cracking the sonic wall from the topside was not the hair-raising adventure it had been to the pioneers, but like knowledge about which end of a gun the bullets come from, it could be unnerving when faced. Doc started to take a deep breath; the breath was half indrawn when he knew already they were into it. There wasn't much doubt. It was like going into the jaws of a gigantic machine operating at crazy speed. Like falling into such a machine if you were a tiny object and as fragile as a penny matchbox. It lasted—well—it was hard to know how long it lasted, because terror was timeless, as it always is, and then they were through and the controls were hard again and the rocket ship all in one piece.

"You all right, Savage?" the pilot asked in a shaken voice.

Doc touched his nose and discovered it was bleeding a little. "All green here," he said. "I think the next time I do that, I'd prefer it be at a higher altitude."

"Oh, brother!" the pilot said. "You and me both. I'll go up to forty thousand before I try it on the return trip."

"Check point?" Doc asked.

"One minus Check Fourteen, sir. Altitude thirty-one thousand. Airspeed five hundred and eighty."

"Cut to three hundred gradually."

"Right!"

10

"Scan for signal," Doc directed.

"Scanner on. Signal spotted. Bearing two-seven-three. Error two-point-five."

"Set blow-sight," Doc said.

"Blow-sight set. All green. Error two-point-five dialed." The pilot apparently swallowed. "Good luck, sir. It's been a privilege, if I may say so."

"Thanks, and good luck," Doc said.

He steeled himself and waited. Three-point-eight-one seconds later, the blow-off sight, which was similar to an automatic bomb sight, functioned and the blister in which he was riding was hurled clear of the ship by an explosive charge.

When the blister had decelerated to the proper point, the automatic toss-out sent the parachutes aloft, and the shock that followed was not bad. After that, there was quite a lot of swinging during a long monotonous fall into the cloud floor.

In the cloud floor, there was anything but monotony. He went in at eighteen thousand, the altimeter in the blister told him, and his eyes told him what he was going into—cumulonimbus. The great nodular stacks of clouds like the intestines out of a monster, with the shipped-away anvil tops meant cumulonimbus, thunderheads, wind, lightning, hail, rain, and trouble. Even big planes avoided such things.

He began to feel the darting and jolting of the nachelle; he watched the rate-of-climb uneasily; in this case the instrument might properly be called a rate-of-fall. As he watched it, it stopped and actually began to climb again; the up-currents inside a thunderhead were frequently terrific. He began to tighten all his muscles, then caught himself showing this nervousness and relaxed.

11

The thunderstorm was not entirely unexpected; even the weather was supposed to be secret behind the Iron Curtain, but the meteorologists were no fools, and they had computed a cold front lying across Moscow. A cold front meant thunderstorms. He had hoped, though, that he wouldn't have to come down through the center of one.

The rate-of-climb needle showed descent again. He watched it, deciding both chutes were still intact and pulling. Losing a chute wouldn't be too bad; there was a reserve for the nachelle, and he wore a pack-chute himself. Every precaution had been taken along that line.

The real danger, the thing that bothered him most, was that the storm might ruin the spot-drop. He was being pinpointed; he had been dropped like a precision-aimed bomb.

Down below on the earth somewhere there was a microwave-beam projector, and the blow-off blister was self-directed automatically and would land somewhere near that. Or would it? The thunderstorm might ruin that.

Rain smeared the plastic blister shell. It made the world a void of grease. Lightning stood out intermittently about him in rods and shaking forks. He could hear the thunder as cannonading. Once there was the ugly clatter of hail against the transparent plastic.

A warning horn began twittering. It was set to operate at three thousand feet above terrain. He consulted gauges quickly; rate of fall was normal, all strain lights were green. He decided not to use the back-pack chute.

He touched the guide-path check-control button. Green. But the orange beside it flickered also. He was, then, not exactly on scheduled descent path, but not too far off it.

He had now a short burst of seconds in which to be tormented by whatever was at hand in his mind to torment him. In other words, he was waiting to hit the ground.

His thoughts went, automatically, to the project as a whole; its magnitude and its significance. These still seemed impressive; they seemed worth the risk he was taking. It was not a nice business, quite likely he was now engaged in the most placid part of it, and he was quite sure this would be the least dangerous portion. But he saw no regrets, and that was important.

He hit.

Good God, I've landed in a river of some sort, he thought. But then, when there was no rolling and tumbling, and after the first wild bouncing and splash a comparative stillness except for the thunder of the rain, he changed the conviction. He had merely hit the edge of a gully or ditch and bounced into it. There was a sensation in his feet and he looked down and saw the faces of the instruments—luminous by radiance—disappear one by one. When he explored with a hand, the hand went into water.

He came out of his inactivity, startled to realize he'd just been sitting there enjoying the novelty of being earthbound again.

His hand located the black-light projector and he pointed it outward and pressed the control. At the same time, he put on the scanner that went with the arrangement for seeing in the dark.

He was sitting like a rather elongated glass egg in a ditch about ten feet deep and not much wider, and the coursing water was about two feet deep. It was raining pitchforks, and the rain didn't help operation of the black-light scanner.

He remained where he was, perfectly attentive to a certain light. It was supposed to flash, controlled by the man who was to meet him here. Presently it did glow. Green.

Throwing open the safety belts, he touched the exit trigger; with a jolt the blister opened almost in two halves. When he stood up, the naturalness of the rain was against his face.

A voice on the ditch edge above addressed him in very good Russian. "*Kak vahse zdarovye, tovarichi?*"

Although it was the equivalent of a "How are you doing, pal?" he jumped violently, then said, "That's a fine greeting. Where is your sense of drama?"

It was Ham Brooks on the ditch edge; he knew that in spite of the darkness. Ham Brooks was one of his group of five aides who had been associated with him almost from the beginning of his career.

"I take it you're all right," Ham said. "Well, I'm not. It's this damn mud. I never knew mud could be so thoroughly mud. Whenever I take a step, I keep expecting it to squirt out of my ears."

Ham's handling of the English language was completely Harvard; it was an oddity about Ham that he spoke a number of foreign languages with completely native accenting, but his English was so affected as to be almost irritating. He was a lawyer by trade. A superior lawyer. But he rarely took time out from the pursuit of excitement to do any court work.

"Coast clear?" Doc Savage asked.

"As far as I can tell," said Ham Brooks. "You missed the zero spot about a hundred and fifty yards. I guess it was that thunderstorm. How was the trip in?"

"Fine," Doc said. "Here, catch this line. I want you to haul up two equipment packs."

The apparatus was in two aluminum cases enclosed in sponge rubber and waterproof plastic film. Ham drew them out of the gully. "Grab the end of the line." Then, when Doc stood beside him, Ham asked, "What about the chariot you arrived in?"

"The dropping blister, you mean? It is auto-timed for demolition in two hours."

"Won't the explosion leave pieces and get attention?"

"No explosion," Doc said. "A Thermit compound. Everything will simply burn up."

"In this rain?"

"All materials entering the structural composition of the blister were impregnated during manufacture. They'll burn, all right, rain or no rain."

Ham suddenly laughed. "Doc, you've no idea how good it is to hear you casually tossing off the incredible. I've been in this dopey country just long enough to forget that your kind of efficiency exists."

"What is the general picture?" Doc asked, interested.

"Not good," Ham said. "There's more bestiality than efficiency. But don't get me wrong—on the side of bestiality, there is plenty of efficiency."

"You're not just speaking as a capitalist?"

"No," Ham said. "I'm speaking as a guy who wishes the human race would come to its senses and stop letting cold-blooded tyrants cut its throat."

"What's your transportation?"

"I have a car," Ham explained. "It's parked in the brush down the way a bit."

"Car? How did you manage that?"

"Monk."

"Oh."

"That part's a long and painful story which I will skip at this point," Ham Brooks explained. "But I think I should break the news to you— hold your hat—that our Lieutenant Colonel Andrew Blodgett "Monk" Mayfair is now a commissar in the Russian Textile Workers' Union. I don't understand exactly what that is, but it can't be as important as he claims it is."

"Monk's status rates him a personal car, eh?"

"And a chauffeur."

"Oh. Where is the chauffeur?"

"It galls my soul to tell any man this," Ham said bitterly. "But the chauffeur stands right in front of you. Me."

"You!"

"Pray to God it may never happen to a dog— yes."

Doc had trouble with a grin. "Hard for you to take, eh?"

"Frankly," said Ham, "rather than put up with the indignity, I have seriously considered letting civilization go right ahead to hell."

3

The car was a Russakoff, and seemed to be a very earnest imitation of one of the best-known American makes, even to body line and radiator grilling. It ran quite well, too—that was because it was a commissar's car, Ham Brooks explained.

They loaded in and drove through squirm-drifting sheets of cold rain over a road that was bumpy and full of abrupt twists and turns. It had also been paved with cobblestones of the general size of washtubs, probably during the reign of Ivan the Terrible.

"About thirty miles to Moscow," Ham said. "We will enter by the Nikos Kaja Ulitza, Ulitza Dsershinskoge Spelenka—that's all one street, to give you an idea of how simple things are around here."

"Do I need any briefing?" Doc asked.

"You'll have more need for the luck of a saint," Ham said. He hesitated, then added, "No, you'll just need to operate in your usual fashion. . . . I tell you, this place runs people nuts, and I'm forgetting just how efficient you can be."

"Let's have some details," Doc said. "Less the around-the-bush technique."

"Nobody takes a straight line in Russia," Ham said. "It gets you to tomorrow too quick. . . . Seriously, though, we've had some good luck and some bad."

17

"How bad?"

"The worst snag," Ham said, "is picking our apple, now that we've found him. I'll skip a lot of the details, some of which have been in your hands for some time, and some of which we felt too vital to chance interception. But the general picture is that there is one official, a central coordinator or whatever you want to call him— one spider who has hold of one end of all the threads that make up the web—who is our answer. If we can grab him, get truth serum and drugs into him, get the facts out of him, get them recorded, and get them back to the part of the world where they know what daylight is, well, we've done our job. His name is Frunzoff."

Doc Savage watched the spongy blobs of pale milk light that the headlamps were pushing over the road. He was impressed.

"Ham, that's a remarkable piece of work in itself," he said. "Nobody, as far as I know, and I've had access to the most confidential reports of several nations, has been able to learn the identity or even the existence of such a spider, as you call him."

Ham Brooks was surprised. "But, hell, you told us that was what we were to look for when we started the job."

"I didn't have a single fact," Doc said. "But it is only logical that Stalin, in view of his phobia about assassination, and its not remote likelihood, would have established a master control responsible only to him, and completely unknown even to his associates in the Kremlin."

"He has. Frunzoff is it."

"Who is Frunzoff? What is his background?"

"That," said Ham, "is what I could be trite and call the sixty-four-dollar question. Frunzoff can be male, female, bird, beast, or catfish, and we would be none the wiser. And not surprised, incidentally."

"You haven't put your finger on Frunzoff, then?"

"No."

"Any leads?"

"Monk claims he has some," Ham said. "I'm not too sure. You know how the big ape is."

Doc said fervently, "I hope his leads aren't female, the way they've been known to be."

"So do I!" Ham said explosively.

"How about that?"

"Well, for Monk, he's been remarkably nonpartial so far," Ham admitted. "I think that this commissar job has let him see enough of the way they do things here to keep him thoroughly scared. He has warned me a dozen times that if there's one slip, we'll all disappear like drops of water on a hot stove."

"That doesn't sound too much like Monk."

"Wait until you see Commissar Michevitch—that's Monk," Ham said, chuckling. "When you've seen that, you've seen something."

Wind struck the car, repeated rushing roaring blows, and the rain made great washings overhead and a sound of a continuous small waterfall under the wheels. There were no streetlights yet. Doc palmed some of the condensation from inside the window, looked out, and decided with astonishment that the number of ramshackle frame huts, typical Russian village *izba*, meant they were in the outskirts of Moscow.

"Any chance of roadblocks and an inspection?" Doc asked.

"I was hoping you wouldn't think of that," Ham told him uneasily. "Sure there is. If it wasn't raining cats and dogs, I would guarantee it. How are you fixed for identification?"

"That's taken care of. I'm Ivar Golat, a messenger for the GPU, the State Political Administration. You don't know me, so in case we're stopped, I'm just a *tovarich* you gave a lift. Where are you quartered?"

"With Monk. On Ulitza Ogarewa."

"That's near the Kremlin."

"A few blocks away."

"Monk will be there?"

"Supposed to be." Ham suddenly slammed on the brakes, changed his mind, blew the horn angrily, and stamped on the accelerator. The performance had no effect on the bedraggled raincoated soldier who stood in their path; he simply pointed his rifle at them. Ham said, "Damn!" and slid the wheels to a stop. "Road check," he told Doc. "Means nothing, probably."

The soldier, a gaunt rough-looking specimen, took his time and worked on their nerves a little; he aimed his rifle with great deliberation, first at Ham, then at Doc, after ostensibly cocking the piece. Then he strolled around to the side of the car and kicked the door.

"*Predooprezhdeneeye?*" he said.

"How in tophet do you expect us to see any warning signs in this rain?" Ham demanded in Russian, thrusting out his head. "And why don't you stay in shelter, you fool?"

The soldier sneered, jerked open the car door,

and popped a flashlight beam inside. He noted the labels on Doc's equipment cases, and the official seals—they were good counterfeits—and he jumped back hastily. *"Mne zhahl!"* he said uneasily. He waved them on.

Ham put the car in motion, and when they had rolled a ways, said, "Decking you out as a messenger for the State Political Administration was a good idea. When he saw the phony seals, he figured you were working, and it scared him into some courtesy."

"Is that a good sample of courtesy?"

"It's the general idea," Ham said. "That guy was probably a security agent. You can generally spot the small-timers like him by their insolence."

There were streetlights now, and a little automobile traffic. Doc could distinguish houses of the czarist era with their pillared porticoes, and here and there a church, usually abutted in close proximity by some large and ugly barrackslike structure which had been built during the antireligious era prior to the German invasion. They were following Ulitza Dsershinskoge, one of the main thoroughfares which wheel-spoked from the Kremlin area on the Moskwareka. The street had a tramway and a busline, and both types of conveyances were incredibly crowded.

Ham made a turn, got on Nikos Kaja Ulitza, and presently he said, "This is a little out of the way, but everybody drives past here once."

They were in Red Square, the area along the Kremlin's somber wall, between the Nikolski and Spaski gates, where was located the Bratskiye Mogili, the Brothers' Graves, where were buried the five hundred revolutionists killed in the

October Revolution, and others added later, including the victims of the explosion of August 25, 1919.

Here was the shrine of Soviet. They could see presently the Lenin Mausoleum, which stood out from the other graves, a somber red structure, designed by an architect named Schuseff in 1924, built first of wood, then made over in stone. At the entrance, spotlighted, were the guards always to be seen there, and the area on the roof where Stalin and high Soviet associates are so often newsreeled while reviewing displays of Soviet pageantry.

Ham saluted the Kremlin wall with a wry "Behind there, presumably, good old Joe is hard at work. They tell me he functions at night, like an owl."

"Let's hope he has no crystal ball in which he sees a couple of Americans with bad intentions in the neighborhood."

Ham chuckled. "I second that with bowed head."

They turned on Red Square, which was approximately a kilometer long, and Ham drove west and across Bewojuzli Place. They began to leave the neighborhood; the old city which had been residential at one time, but was now taken over by the offices of Soviet bureaucrats.

Ham Brooks saw Doc Savage's hand at the open window, frowned, and said, "You toss something out?"

"Yes."

"What?"

"Just some stuff. A powder."

Ham grinned uneasily. "You've done it three or

four times, haven't you? Think we're being followed?"

"It would be worth knowing if we were," Doc said.

"If you want to see a man jump squarely out of a perfectly good skin, just let me find out we're being followed," Ham said.

The street where Ham and Monk were living had a tired grimy age about it, as if the dead years had been stacked there to wait out eternity. Ham turned the car into what had once been a coach entrance, first alighting to unlock large iron-strapped doors, and Doc waited until the lights were off and the engine dead. Then he removed his equipment cases and followed Ham up a succession of worn steps.

"Monk will sure be glad to see you," Ham said. "He has been putting up a big front about not worrying." Ham came to a door, winked at Doc, then gave the door a kicking and said in a vicious guttural voice completely unlike his own, "Security police! Come out with your hands up, son of a capitalist!"

Monk wore a considerable grin during the first thirty seconds of waiting; then he lost the pleased expression slowly.

Doc said dryly, "You fellows are still pulling practical jokes on each other, I take it."

Ham grimaced. "I wonder if I scared the big lug so bad he jumped out of a window?" He inserted a key in the lock, turned it, and called prudently, "Take it easy, you missing link. Our visitor's here," before he pushed into the room. Then he looked around, said, "Hey, where are you, Monk?" He ran into the kitchen and bedroom. "He

23

doesn't seem to be here," Ham said, and alarm made his voice a little higher.

"Would that be serious?" Doc asked sharply.

"If he's not getting back at me for that gag, it's serious," Ham said. "He was going to be here." Ham began a second tour of the apartment, which was furnished with almost painful sparseness. "I don't know what to do about this," he said.

"Let's check to see whether we were followed," Doc said. He opened one of the equipment cases, took out a small vial, glanced at Ham, and asked, "One of us will have to saunter out into the street. You belong in the neighborhood, so maybe you'd better do it."

"What in blazes do I look for?"

"Got a cold?"

"No."

"All right. Take a sniff of this." Doc uncorked the small glass vial and passed it to Ham.

"Quite a perfume," Ham said, puzzled. "A little different from anything I ever smelled before."

Doc told him, "Just go out in the street and cross it a couple of times. See if you detect the identical odor. It's distinctive enough that you won't make an error. But it will not be very strong."

Ham was gone from the apartment not quite five minutes, and he came back wearing alarm.

"It's in the street, faintly," he said. "What in the devil is it?"

Doc named the chemicals. "You're not a chemist, so that may not mean much. But several times during the trip in from where I landed, I tossed small quantities of two different chemical concoctions out on the road. One type at one point, and the other a couple of hundred feet farther on. The wheels of any machine following us would pick up one, then the other—the two when combined cause that odor."

"Good God!" Ham blurted. "Then we were followed!"

"It isn't positive," Doc warned. "It could have been another car accidentally following our course part of the way."

"Maybe, but the way I buy it, it scares me." Ham yanked a suitcase out and began dumping clothing into it. "Let's get out of here."

4

Doc Savage slid over the edge of the window-sill and poised there a moment, supported by the grip of his bronze fingers, while he told Ham, "I'll leave the cord in place, in case you want to come out in a hurry by the same route. If it's an ambush, both front and back doors will be watched, and they might watch this route too. So be careful."

Ham shuddered and said, "I remember climbing down that cord one time. I'd about as soon jump. Be careful yourself."

The cord was silk and there were knots at eighteen-inch intervals, and at every third knot there was a small attached loop which could be of use. To one end of the cord was affixed a small folding grapple hook. The whole thing was a somewhat childish gimmick, and certainly primitive except for the excellence of the workmanship, but Doc Savage was convinced that the thing had saved his life more than once in the past, so he always carried it. He descended to an alley court below, and although he did not seem to expend much effort, climbing or descending the cord was, as Ham had indicated, not an easy feat.

He had made no perceptible noise, and now he moved quietly along a wall, beginning to feel a little silly about the precautions, and shoved his head around a corner, almost against the back of a man who was standing against the wall, doing his best to make himself part of it. A nice quick dividend for caution, Doc thought, wondering if he could ever start breathing again.

Considering that the man was all of twelve inches from Doc's eyes, he seemed a remarkably vague figure. Doc withdrew around the corner with all of the reckless haste of a snail in heavy going. Then he tried to decide whether the man was really nine feet tall and bristling with machine guns. Probably not. Thank God for the thickness of the night, though.

The important thing was that the fellow had been looking in the other direction. Doc waited. He could hear the other taking the long halting breaths of a man doing a nerve-racking job that was going too slowly.

That lasted two or three minutes, then Doc heard footsteps. The watcher heard them too; he promptly stepped back around the corner, which put him where Doc had been standing an instant before.

It was very dark. The rain had stopped falling, but water still dripped from eaves. Everyone and everything seemed to be listening and straining.

"Seryi!"

The footsteps stopped.

"Psssst! Seryi!" This from the watcher who had all but backed into Doc bodily.

"F chom d'la?" asked a woman's pleasant voice. "What is the matter, Mahli?"

"It is you, Seryi?"

"Of course."

"Ah, good. No one has left by this route. How long do I have to stand here in the infernal rain?"

"It has stopped raining, Mahli."

"It will start again. How long do I have to stay here?"

"No longer. You may go now, Mahli."

The word *mahli* was Russian for "little" or "small," and the girl Seryi was using it in a manner that indicated a dry humor, Doc concluded. The fellow Mahli was only slightly smaller than a tank, Doc reflected, watching him stalk off without another word.

He waited for some sign from the woman. There was none. Apparently she was standing perfectly still. Then a long ruffianly gobble of thunder came from the dark bowels of the sky, and a sudden shotting of rain fell. Feet clicked lightly, and Doc recoiled. The woman Seryi had chosen the same shelter as the man: she stood almost against Doc.

Having weighed everything, Doc put out a hand all cupped to go over the girl's mouth.

Seryi was somewhat taller than he thought, and so he got hold of her throat at first; finally he had to tighten down on the columnar softness of her neck to preserve some silence. A few things—the smoothness of her skin, her activity, the swiftness of her reactions—indicated a young woman. He was also kicked, scratched, and had some hair loosened. He said, in Russian fortunately, "*Teek-ha!*" He said it twice. Then she stopped kicking, scratching, and hair-yanking. She was very still in his grip.

He repeated the word for quietly again. "*Teek-ha!*" Then he asked, "Will you scream if I release you?"

She shook her head vigorously no.

"Will you give sensible answers?" he asked.

Her head moved to indicate yes.

He removed his hands warily. "All right. Who are you?"

"Seryi," she said.

"I don't mean your name," he said.

She turned around and gave him the jackpot. "Mr. Savage, you and Mr. Brooks must get out of here in a hurry," she said. "It's very important. You are in definite danger here."

Doc took a moment to recover. "Who do you think I am?" he asked cautiously.

"Stand here and play guessing games!" She stamped a foot. "Let the secret police show up! Then have guessing games!" She reached out and gripped his arm. "Oh, I'm doing this all wrong. Monk Mayfair sent me."

"Who?"

"I was in a car waiting near the Minin and Pozharski monument on Red Square," she said. "I was supposed to spot your car, but I didn't. I missed it. I drove into this street and turned and drove back again, and waited at the corner awhile. I didn't see your car, concluded you had arrived, and came around to tell Mahli I would take over—"

"Who is Mahli?" Doc asked. "Besides being the human tank who just left here."

"Mahli? My cousin. I asked him to help me." She was speaking in a low, excited voice. Suddenly Doc turned his flashlight beam on her face for a moment. It was a very sweet face and surprisingly composed. She gasped at the light, said, "I hope you're satisfied."

"I'm satisfied you're very good-looking," Doc

said. "Unfortunately, that's about the size of it. Who is this Monk Mayfair?"

"Your caginess is a little childish," she said bitterly. "Mr. Savage, Monk Mayfair discovered the secret police suspected something. Monk couldn't come here. He would be seized. He sent me to intercept you and take you to him. What could be simpler than that?"

"Almost anything would be simpler," Doc said. "Come inside."

They reentered the house via the back door, and Ham listened with astonishment to the pretty Russian girl's story. "You can take us to Monk?" he asked suspiciously.

"Not tomorrow or next month," Seryi said angrily. "I might if you accompany me at once."

Ham looked at Doc unhappily. "You know Monk and his reaction to a pretty face. I thought he was cured, but maybe he wasn't."

"I think," said Seryi, "I should resent that very bitterly."

Doc asked Seryi, "You actually saw Monk recently? Is that your story?"

"Yes," she said. "Of course."

"When?"

"Tonight."

"By any chance, did Monk shake hands with you?" Doc asked speculatively.

"I don't recall Monk shaking my hand," Seryi said. And then she flushed. "But I do think he held both of them for awhile."

Ham laughed bitterly. "I believe she knows Monk, all right."

"Let's see your hands," Doc said. He did nothing but hold the girl's hands for a moment, then

31

release them. But Ham Brooks broke out a relieved expréssion.

Puzzled, Seryi asked, "What is that perfume? It's quite distinctive, isn't it? We don't have much contact with perfume here in Russia, but I like it."

The car to which Seryi led them was quite old, and parked some distance down the street. Doc, eyeing the machine, doubted very much that it would run; they did have trouble starting it, the battery being down. Doc used the crank that Seryi pushed into his hands. He gathered, from the way she gave instructions, that she was quite familiar with the wreck.

"To rate a car, even a clunker like this one, you must be someone rather important," Ham said suspiciously.

"I am a secretary in the Supreme Council of National Economy," Seryi said curtly. "And it is a very dependable car. It is much superior to walking."

The machine began to shake all of its loose parts. Doc tossed the crank in the back and got in. "What has happened to Monk?"

"I told you, Mr. Savage. He suspects they have become suspicious of him."

"What I probably meant," Doc said, "is how did he happen to send a girl, a strange girl at that, with such an important message?"

"I would say it was very logical. He had to send a messenger who would not be suspected."

"And you wouldn't be suspected."

She nodded. "Not by the secret police." She glanced wryly at Doc. "But by you, I think I am very suspect."

"You blame me?"

Seryi drove the old car at a sedate pace. It held together, although it seemed to gather itself and leap with a great clatter over some of the rougher places in the street.

"I think I'd better tell you two things," she said. "First is about my brother, Ancil—he is supposed to have left his life when a Soviet plane crashed in the Nazi territory near the end of the war, but actually he walked away from the crash quite alive and made his way by means of a great effort to New York City, where he is now married, at peace with the US Immigration Bureau, and very happy in his work as a dance instructor in the theater. That is the first thing. The second thing is that my brother Ancil met Mr. Monk Mayfair in New York in the course of some interest which Mr. Mayfair showed in the theater—"

"In the chorus girls, probably," Doc said.

"Well, I would say so too," Seryi said, smiling slightly. "Anyway, my brother Ancil asked Mr. Mayfair to look me up if he ever traveled through Moscow, and Mr. Mayfair did so. That is how I met Mr. Mayfair."

"Is that why you're doing this?"

"It is one reason," she said. "I am most grateful to know my brother is alive and well—and quite glad, also, that the secret police don't know about it. If they did—poof. Off to Siberia I would go."

"The other reason?"

"I will be frank about that, too," Seryi said. "I would like to make a friend who could whisk me away to America."

"That would interest Monk, too," Ham said sourly.

"There is one more thing," Seryi explained.

"What's that?"

"I am to tell you that Frunzoff has one gold tooth and lives at Seven Botsch Bronnaja Ulitza," Seryi said. "That means nothing to me. But Monk asked me to tell you."

Doc Savage had the impression that he had been hit squarely between the eyes with a hammer; he was so surprised that his head began aching. He heard Ham, beside him, resume breathing with an effort. "My God!" Ham gasped. "Monk must have been busier than a clamdigger!"

"The name means something to you?" Seryi asked.

"What name was that?" Ham asked warily.

"Frunzoff."

Ham hesitated only a moment, then lied glibly, "Not a thing, I'm sorry to say. And I'm surprised Monk would ask you to pass along something like that. Let's see—could it be code? But I can't imagine what kind of code."

"Mr. Mayfair was very excited," Seryi said. "So it could be some kind of code, perhaps."

"What excited Monk?"

"Danger, I imagine. As a matter of fact, Mr. Mayfair was dreadfully upset."

On a rising alarm, Ham said, "That doesn't sound good. Normally Monk wouldn't be upset with a wildcat in each hip pocket."

"He was particularly emphatic that I should tell you of Frunzoff," the girl said.

"What address was that again?" Doc inquired.

"On the Botsch Bronnaja Ulitza, number seven."

"I see."

"Do you know where that is?"

"It's a little beyond Twerskoj Boulevard," Doc said. "That right?"

"Yes."

Doc became silent. He was inclined to mentally damn Monk for giving this girl the Frunzoff name. Frunzoff, the way Ham had explained it, was the key to the whole elaborate plot. Frunzoff was the man they wanted—therefore it was vitally important that nobody know that they wanted Frunzoff. Their scheme was intricate, and included getting the information they wished out of Frunzoff without even Frunzoff knowing it had happened. Doc glanced at Ham when they passed a streetlight, and Ham's face was a mask of alarm. Monk was in desperate straits, Ham believed.

Doc leaned forward and tapped the girl's shoulder. "Where are you taking us?"

"To Mr. Mayfair," she said.

"Be more specific."

She hesitated. Her shoulders rose and fell. "It's my apartment, as a matter of fact."

Ham whistled softly—and got his face slapped. The girl's hand flew out; the whack of her palm against Ham's cheek was a sharp sound. "Hey!" Ham blurted. "You little tramp—" The girl began to sob, and the car swerved. Doc reached over and grasped the wheel. "Easy on the temperament," he said.

"Damn you, I'm not—what do you call it?—a tramp," Seryi sobbed angrily. Then she looked up, her face became much more distorted, and she screamed, "Watch out! The secret police!"

Doc had already seen the car, an old-fashioned job with a squarish body, a sedan. It had come up beside and moved out to pass them; now it made a lunge at their front wheels, and Doc had a moment when he felt sure that the old car was beefed up with armor plate around the fenders. It was too late for the notion to be of any help, because the police car promptly hit them.

There was no siren, no shouting. The machine just hit them. Their front wheels held together, but a tie rod snapped. The car went out of control, took a crazy lunge to the left, then to the right, and smashed into the rear of the assailant machine. The latter car, knocked crosswise of the road, skidded a few yards and rolled over on its side. Men spilled out as their own car came to a crazy stop.

Doc gripped Seryi's shoulder, asked, "Know which way is south?"

"Yes! But they're armed! We haven't a chance—"

"Run south," Doc said. "Don't argue. Two blocks, then turn on Glinischt Street. We'll overtake you there." To Ham he said, "I'm going to use smoke on them."

The street winked redly twice with flame from a gun muzzle. Doc fumbled for a moment in his clothing, seeking the gadget he wanted, then found it and let fly. It was a smoke grenade, cylindrical, not much more than an oversized Fourth of July firecracker in size. It landed in the street and made very little sound letting go, hardly any sound at all, but produced a great deal of astonishingly black smoke. The stuff started as a dark melon, became progressively a sheep, a calf, a horse, a small house in size.

There was another shot in what was now complete blackness. "*Net! Net! Net!*" an excited Russian voice said. "*Smatreete!*" There was no more shooting after the warning.

Doc, very loudly in Russian also, said, "There is a fire!" There was no fire in the sense he hoped they would think, but they might believe for a moment the smoke was coming from a burning car.

He began retreating, and came out of the smoke. In a moment, another figure stumbled out of the blackness. Ham. They ran away from the spot as quietly as possible.

Doc looked ahead, saw no sign of Seryi, and Ham was evidently doing the same thing, because Ham whispered, "Good Lord, she's fast on her feet to get out of sight."

They lengthened their stride now. They came to Glinischt Street, turned into it. They stopped.

"She isn't here. She didn't run for it," Doc said grimly. "She wasn't harmed. I told her exactly what to do."

"I heard you," Ham said. "I can't understand what could have gone wrong." He turned and stepped back into the street where the smoke was. His dive for cover was phenomenal, accompanied by a crashing of pistol fire.

"Don't be a fool," Doc said.

Ham shuddered. "Now you tell me! . . . I think they're running away themselves, though."

"What?"

"Take a look. I don't mean stick your head into the street; for God's sake, don't do that. But you've got that mirror gimmick, haven't you?"

The mirror gimmick was more or less conventional, a mirror attached with a swivel to a telescoping rod affair. Not the best sort of periscope, but compact. Doc, examining the street by thrusting the thing around the corner, felt that it left a great deal to be desired. But it showed him a great deal to be puzzled with.

"They've got the girl?" Ham asked, carefully getting nowhere near the corner.

"Yes, I think so. . . . You're right about their flight, too. They're leaving. In a hurry. And not coming this direction."

"That's odd," Ham muttered. "For secret police, that's a mighty odd move."

Doc asked dryly, "You think they are secret police?"

"No more than you do," Ham said bitterly. "Doc, we're being foxed. This was arranged. That girl didn't flee because she didn't want to."

"It wasn't an assassination attempt," Doc said. "It went through the motions of one, but there was no steam behind it."

"Could the whole object have been to give the girl a chance to leave us?"

"Maybe. A trifle elaborate, though, wouldn't you say?"

"It has me stumped."

"No, I think you got the essential point," Doc said thoughtfully. "The girl made contact with us, gave us Frunzoff's address, and with her job done, she was removed from our clutches, so to speak, in a way that might let her be useful to them again later."

"In other words, we're supposed to think she's what she said she was, a girl very grateful because she has a brother happily in New York?"

"I'm guessing about that," Doc confessed. "I don't like the guess too well. She seemed a decent sort."

"They always do. . . . What about Frunzoff?"

"Did you bring one of the equipment cases?"

Ham said, "Yes." He went to a niche and produced the case. "You've got the other, I see. . . . Does this mean we go to that address and try for Frunzoff?"

"We've got to," Doc said. "There's too much at stake to be cautious."

5

Number seven on Botsch Bronnaja Ulitza was one of those low aristocratic mansion houses with pillar-porticoes against a background of church cupolas and a few modernistic boxes of buildings turned shockingly ugly by city grime. They reached it to the accompaniment of an appropriate display by the weather—thunder ran thumping through the narrow street and rain began falling in bucketfuls.

"What the devil do we do now?" Ham asked gloomily. "Walk in? That's crazy, isn't it? I wish we knew what happened to Monk."

Doc found a niche which afforded some shelter from the downpour. "Let's use our heads a little before we get in any deeper," he said. "First, about Monk: either they've got him, or he's alarmed and hiding out. The girl said he was hiding out in her apartment."

Ham blew rainwater off his lips. "I don't believe a word she said."

"Does Monk have two-way radio?"

"Yes, but that's not going to help. We found out one thing—the Communists have electronic monitors that scan every wavelength automatically, and the moment an unauthorized signal goes on, a receiver is thrown on that frequency. We haven't dared use radio."

"What about alternate hideouts?" Doc asked.

"We have two. But Monk wouldn't be—or would he?" Ham swore gently. "Damn! Do you suppose I've overlooked the obvious answer to his whereabouts?"

"How far are these hideouts?"

"Not so very far. We bunched them, figuring we might want to get from one to another in a hurry. One is on Nastass, the other farther out."

"Go check them," Doc said.

"Now?" Ham gasped.

"Yes."

Ham hesitated, then said gloomily, "Who do you think you're fooling? You're trying to get me out of here in case it's a trap."

"I'm not trying to fool you," Doc said quickly. "I do want you away from here in case it's an ambush. And why not? If they get all of us, the whole project is shot. And I'm also worried about Monk, and want to locate him if he's free."

"Is that an order?" Ham asked bitterly. "If it's not, the devil with it."

"It's an order, Ham."

"You can guess what I think of it," Ham said. "But all right. Where will you meet me?" Ham gave the address on Nastass Ulitza, and another farther out in the suburbs on a street called Corski. "They're just rooms we rented. Will you try them?"

Doc indicated the house where Seryi had said the man known as Frunzoff lived. "My work in there will take at least two hours."

Ham shivered. "You think you can do it single-handed?"

"I can try."

Ham said, "I've argued with you before. . . . I'll be back here, then, provided I have a potful of luck."

When Ham had sidled warily away and was lost in the blinding rain, Doc Savage unscrewed the mirror from the small telescoping rod which had held it, and now he had about eighteen inches of hollow tubing. The diameter of this, at the small end, was not much more than a darning needle. To the large end, he attached a small rubber bulb which he first filled with colorless liquid from a small flask which he kept unsealed no longer than was absolutely necessary. During this operation, and particularly while the flask was open, he held his breath, and after that he was careful to carry the tube with the filled bulb attached well to the lee so that the lunging wind would whip the fumes away from him.

Now he moved brazenly on the sidewalk, walking openly and directly to the house. Three stone steps led up to the garish portico, and he mounted them quickly.

He stood beside the door, felt for the lock, located the keyhole, inserted the end of his hollow-tube gadget, and gave the bulb a long slow squeeze. He held his breath during this operation, and not until he stepped away from the vicinity of the door did he resume normal breathing.

A passageway, carriage-width, separated this house from the adjacent one, and he walked into that, reloading the syringe affair as he went. There was a door at the back, but it had no lock or keyhole that he could find; evidently it was secured by a bar inside. He knelt down and tried the point of the tube under the door, and it would pass. He emptied the bulb again.

If there had been a sound in the house, the whooping of thunder and the beating rush of the rain had blanketed it.

Back at the front door again, he used a lock pick for a few moments. That got the door open about six inches—as far as a chain inside would let it swing. He tinkered with the chain for awhile and got nowhere.

He used a Thermitlike compound on the chain; a bead of it which he quickly embedded in a sticky pellet that would ignite it presently by chemical reaction, and which also served as an adhesive to hold the Thermit to the steel chain. He closed the door and waited.

The stuff burned through the chain briefly. He could see traces of the glare around the edge of the closed door, and inside the house the display must have been blinding. But it was quicker than fooling around with a hacksaw. The stuff was, in effect, a chemical substitute for a cutting torch.

He opened the door and stepped inside. In chairs on each side of the door sat men with thick bodies and heavy faces, uniformed, with submachine guns on their laps.

Doc Savage looked thoughtfully at the two guards. Presently he said in a voice of normal loudness, *"Slyshyte lee vy menyah?"* When they did not stir, he repeated the same thing amiably in English, "Do you hear me?" No response.

He reached out and put a finger against one of the heavy narrow foreheads and shoved lightly.

The guard toppled and would have fallen had Doc not caught him quickly and righted him. "Nice nap, boys," he said cheerfully, and went quickly to the rear of the house.

There were two more guards at a back door. There was one at a window. All were in chairs, and all slept from the effects of the anesthetic gas he had introduced with the syringe gadget.

The house had three floors, and the downstairs area had been severely plain. He found a staircase and began climbing; at the top he found another guard, this one lying on the floor and breathing heavily through his nose.

Now the furnishings changed suddenly from drab to utter luxury; he was walking on a carpet that seemed to brush his ankles, passing mirrors in great gilt frames and oil paintings which were museum pieces. The paintings startled him. He saw a Veronese, two Van der Weydens, a Michelangelo, a Rubens, a Gainsborough which he suspected was a copy but which might not be.

He began to wear a frown, and back of it was an excitement rising and tightening. At a rough guess there was a round two million dollars' worth of paintings here in the hall, and that did not seem the stuff that a trap would be made of.

Frunzoff, as they understood it, was the faceless nonentity who, if anything happened to Stalin, would suddenly become number-one man. Frunzoff, then, would be the one man Stalin had decided to trust; he was the receptacle for all the centralized knowledge to which Stalin and no one else had access. Such a man would be important. He would be likely to have a couple of million in old masters hanging in his hall.

He began using the syringe gadget on doors. There were three doors opening off the hall, all closed. He went to each in turn, working rapidly. The anesthetic gas, colorless and odorless, was one that he had developed a long time ago. It produced quick unconsciousness, and the period of stupor could be varied by changing the ingredients. The formula he was using now ensured about three hours of coma. The effect occurred entirely within the first minute of release; after that it went through an oxidizing process with the oxygen in the air and became harmless. That was why he was holding his breath.

He tried the doors. Two were unlocked. The first of these let him into a conference room, the second into an office. He leaped to a desk here and noticed that his hands were made a little unsteady by excitement as he searched. The name was Frunzoff, all right. But Frunzoff was the first name. The second was Nosh. Frunzoff Nosh. "Nosh" meant "knife" in the Russian language, which might be significant.

He used his lock pick on the third door, and stepped inside. The sitting room was enormous. There was a Gobelin on the wall; the rug was a priceless Oriental that dated back to Crusade days. He passed through a door.

For a moment he looked down at the man who slept on a great silly bed that was all of twelve feet square and placed in the center of the room on a raised dais. The man wore silk. Everything in the room that could be silk was silk, and it was all one shade of bird's-egg blue.

The man himself would have fitted better in monk's cloth, but not in a monastery. He was a frame of great bones with dark leathery hide that good living had softened and diseases had pocked and stained slightly. The one homely touch was his false teeth; they rested in a glass of water beside the bed, like anybody's false teeth.

Doc placed his equipment cases on a table. In a moment, he went to the bed and gave the man— if there was a Frunzoff Nosh here, this was he— the first administration of truth serum.

This part of the plan was direct enough. Frunzoff was unconscious from the anesthetic, but the bridge-over into twilight coma could be secured with a stimulant administered simultaneously with the sodium-amytal formula he intended to use. It should not take too long.

Waiting for the medicinal reaction, he set up the small portable wire recorder, gave it a test run, and adjusted the audio gain.

He said into the microphone, "This is Clark Savage, speaking from number seven Botsch Bronnaja Ulitza, in Moscow." He consulted his watch, gave the hour, minute, and the date. He added, "I have gained admission to the house, which I have reason to believe is occupied by a Russian official named Frunzoff Nosh, for the purpose of questioning the man while he is under the effects of truth serum." He gave a brief description of the house and means of gaining entrance, not because the information was of much record value, but because he was waiting for Frunzoff to respond to the chemicals, and the recording might add authenticity.

He shut off the recorder suddenly. . . . There had been a sound downstairs. He whipped to the door, listened, heard nothing, and then made for a moment a low trilling sound that had once been a rather peculiar habit, a thing he did in moments of intense excitement, but which he had broken himself of making. It was done deliberately now, as a means of identification.

"Doc!" Ham Brooks's voice came sharply from below.

"Yes?" Doc said. "What is it? What about Monk?"

Monk's own voice, a small raspy affair, answered that. "What the devil kind of a joint is this?" Monk demanded.

"Monk, are you all right?"

"I'm more confused than I've been in some time," Monk said. He and Ham came leaping up the stairs. They saw the paintings, and Monk said, "For crying out loud! Are those daubings *real?*"

Doc asked, "What happened to you?"

"I got a telephone call earlier tonight," Monk explained wryly. "I was advised to get the heck out of the place where I was waiting for you and Ham. I figured it was good advice, particularly since it scared the devil out of me. The voice on the telephone seemed to know too much."

"Who called?" Doc demanded.

"Search me."

"A woman?"

"No. Man's voice. I never heard it before, that I recall."

Doc Savage concentrated for a moment, recalling the man named Mahli who had waited for the girl Seryi in the rear of the house where they had first gone. Doc then spoke a few words, imitating Mahli's voice with remarkable fidelity. "That sound anything like it?"

"That's the guy," Monk said, amazed. "Who is he?"

"A girl named Seryi said he was her cousin."

"Who is this Seryi?"

"Don't you know?"

"Never heard of her," Monk said. He added with the air of a man misunderstood, "I haven't made a pass at a babe since I've been here. I've turned over a new leaf."

Ham snorted. "I'd call that a whole book."

"I went to the other hideout, and Ham showed up," Monk explained. "Now, what goes on? I thought this whole thing was supposed to be the biggest secret since Pearl Harbor."

Ham laughed. Monk was not built to register confusion in any but a comical way. His height was a little over five feet, his width not much less, and his homeliness was almost preposterous. His forehead was about a single finger width, and he bore in no respect any resemblance to an eminent chemist, which he was.

"Fan out your ears, and I'll tell you what happened," Ham advised him. "Then you're really going to be bewildered."

Doc Savage did not use hypodermics for the drug, but a mechanical means of administration which resembled in a dwarf form the setup for delivering intravenous saline dosage. His equipment had been prepared in advance; the whole theme had been aimed at what was happening now—to get hold of the man who would know what they wanted to know, drug him, and extract the information.

Frunzoff suddenly heaved, moaned, then gave

an explosion of Russian words. He was cursing. Delirium, and he was reliving some particularly tight moment in his past.

"Hold him down," Doc said. "He's in the middle stage now, and we'll be ready to work on him in a few seconds."

Monk and Ham listened to the man's babbling. Ham said in amazement, "You hear that? He has killed someone, and he's reporting to a superior that he did it. Someone named Uritsky. I seem to have heard that name."

Doc frowned. "Uritsky was a terrorist leader killed during the early days of the Soviet. He was supposedly murdered by the opposition—but the opposition didn't win, and if this fellow killed Uritsky, it was part of a plot to stir up trouble and to get Uritsky out of the way. That sort of thing has been done before."

"Nice guys," Monk said.

"The recorder on?" Ham asked.

"Yes. . . . Ham, you've got the general picture, and you have some experience at cross-examination. Suppose you start the ball rolling."

Ham nodded. "Fine by me." He leaned over Frunzoff and began the casual questioning that they had found it was best to employ to lead into more important matters. Even the drug was not completely effective on a mind suddenly jabbed with a vital question. "What is your name?" Ham asked.

The man mumbled that it was Frunzoff Nosh. He gave his age when Ham asked for it. Fifty-seven. Was he a party member? He was. For how long? Since 1916. Had he known Lenin? Yes. Did he know Stalin? Yes. How well? Quite well. What wās his present connection with Stalin? He was Stalin's coordinator.

Doc Savage said, "Develop that coordinator thing a bit farther with questions. It will help background what we are after."

Ham asked half a dozen questions, then added a comment which summed up Frunzoff's general job.

"Hatchet boy for the head guy," Ham said.

"I'll take it now," Doc said. He replaced Ham beside Frunzoff, and asked quietly, "Frunzoff, you have general information concerning all Soviet preparations for war?"

"*Da*," the man mumbled.

Because the word "truth serum" as applied to the chemical they were using was a misnomer—there was no chemical magic which would make anyone speak the truth and nothing but the truth—it was necessary to keep a continuous barrage of questions going. The man was literally without consciousness; he could not reason, would not remember what had happened afterward in any coherent fashion, but since he was without the capacity to reason, skillful guiding through the drug-induced delirium would produce remarkable results.

"Have you the atom bomb?" Doc asked.

Forty-five minutes later, Doc Savage turned to the microphone and gave the chemical composition of the drugs that had been used, and finished, "This concludes the interview with Frunzoff. All that remains now is to get back to Washington with it."

He switched off the recorder, removed the spool

of wire, and put it in a chamois-lined case. Then he looked up at Monk's and Ham's pale, drawn faces.

"Rather shocking to find it out, wasn't it?" Doc suggested grimly.

"Blazes!" Monk moistened dry lips. "I don't think I ever spent forty-five minutes that scared me worse."

Ham cleared his throat. "That plant near Kazan, where they're processing the Polish uranium—I wish we'd gotten a better description of its location and the method they're using."

"I don't think the man has the technical knowledge to help much there," Doc explained. "As for the location, that's definite. General Staff in Washington knows about that plant—but, I'm quite alarmed to say, they don't have any notion at all that about three-quarters of the others exist."

Monk stared. "The hell! I always suspected the top brass in our army of having the same stuff in their heads that's on their shoulders. But you'd think with all the espionage they've been doing, they'd have more than a child's portion of information."

Doc shook his head. "It has been too well covered. I'll make you a bet that no one outside of Stalin and this fellow here has the information on the Soviet's atomic-warfare status that we just recorded."

Ham looked at the unconscious Frunzoff, scowling. "You know, it's too bad we're partly civilized. A little overdose of the drug would stop that devil's heart and close the lid on a lot of scheming."

"It's an idea," Monk said.

Doc had finished recasing his equipment. "I imagine that will take care of itself, once this recording unwinds through a loudspeaker at a United Nations session. Which is what I hope will ultimately happen. And I believe it will."

"First," Ham said dryly, "we've got to get out of Russia with that thing."

6

Doc Savage produced half a dozen small glass ampuls and divided them among Monk and Ham, keeping one for himself. "Break one of these in your handkerchief and hold it to the nostrils of each guard," he instructed. "In other words, give it about the same way you would chloroform. A minute and a half to two minutes of administration should be sufficient."

"They're knocked out already," Ham said. "Why give them an extra shot of this stuff, whatever it is? Incidentally, what is it?"

"Merely another type of anesthetic," Doc explained. "One that can be counteracted quickly by a stimulant in vapor form."

"Oh, so they'll all wake up about the same time?"

"That's it," Doc agreed. "The information is important, but covering up the fact that we have it is just about as essential. Because of the way the anesthetic sneaks up on you, and the complete lack of aftereffects, nobody here is going to realize what happened. If we're lucky, of course. The anesthetic gas is almost unknown. I'm sure no one here in the house realizes the stuff exists. The guards and Frunzoff will simply wake up, perhaps feel a little puzzled, then think no more of it. Frunzoff, of course, was asleep and will never know

what happened. The guards will conclude they
dropped off to sleep, and the penalty a Russian
guard gets for sleeping on duty is going to keep
them quiet."

Ham Brooks indicated Frunzoff. "Yeah, but you
used a needle on his arm three times. You can see
the bumps that were raised. A guy who took all
the precautions he took is going to ask a doctor
what the devil happened to his arm."

Doc shook his head. "I've prepared for that, I
hope."

"How?"

Doc got a small container, ventilated, from the
equipment case. "I'm a little self-conscious about
the childishness of this one," he said.

He opened the container and released about
three dozen ordinary fleas on Frunzoff's person.

Ham laughed heartily. Monk looked startled and
asked, "What did you do? Take a vacuum cleaner
to a dog?"

"To that pet pig, Habeas Corpus, that you keep
in New York, if you must know," Doc said.

"If they're fleas off that ghastly hog," Ham
Brooks said, "they'll have Frunzoff half-eaten by
morning. He'll never notice a few little things like
hypodermic-needle punctures."

"Check over everything to make sure there is
no sign that we were here," Doc directed.

"When are you going to release the stuff that
will revive them?" Monk asked.

"On the way out. Which will be in a couple of
minutes, I guess."

Doc Savage looked up and down the street, then
stepped through the door and moved aside to let

Monk and Ham pass. He closed the door and made sure the spring lock clicked. He stood there a moment, mentally checking to be sure things inside were as they had found them—no furniture displaced, the same lights on that had been on; there was a multitude of small things that could go amiss, and any one was important if it aroused suspicion.

He moved down the steps. The rain had changed suddenly to sleet, and it was a great deal colder than it had been. The cold front had passed, but before morning there was likely to be quite a lot of sleet and perhaps some snow, according to the predictions of the meteorologists in the American zone.

Monk and Ham had gone to a small sedan of a make popular in Germany prior to the war.

"Stolen car?" Doc asked dubiously.

"No, it's one I chiseled off Trans-Caucasian Soviet Federation, and cached for an emergency," Monk explained. "I figured this was an emergency."

"It's not one the police will be looking for, then?"

Monk hesitated. "I don't see why they would be. I hate to run my neck out too far, though. This Seryi babe and her pal Mahli bobbing up in the picture sort of makes an unbeliever out of me."

"Has anyone the least idea who Seryi and Mahli are?" Doc asked.

No one did have. Monk put the little car into motion, and immediately began to have trouble with the icy street.

Doc Savage was silent, thinking about the situation. The first leg of the project—getting into Moscow and extracting the atomic-warfare-status information from the one man in Russia who probably came nearest to having it all—had gone off, everything considered, not too badly. Doc felt some satisfaction about that. Back of tonight's operation lay several months of careful preparation; Monk had been in Russia since early last summer, and Ham almost as long. The fact that all the facilities of the United States government, and those of most of the other nations allied against world chaos, had been available did not mean it had been easily done. Monk could probably attest to that, and Ham as well.

The information on the record wire was fabulously important. It was, Doc imagined, as vital to the future of world security as anything could be; certainly it was data that would definitely weigh the balance of peace or war. That made it a matter affecting many lives. Not a few hundred or a few thousand lives, but millions—all of the millions who would be drafted into the next conflict.

Specifically, the wire held—he could feel its slight weight in his pocket, a presence almost intangible for such weird importance—the full facts of Soviet atomic work. The locations of all plants, the parts being manufactured in specific places, the whereabouts of the storage depots, and the master plan of Communist operations—all of that was on the wire.

There wasn't the slightest doubt in Doc's mind but that within a week or ten days after the wire was unspooled through a reproducer before the United Nations security organization, the whole disease of totalitarian aggression, which the previous world conflict had failed so piteously to end, would be a dead duck.

Viewed from another point, he had the life and future of every Communist dictator and satellite in his pocket. The minute he got out of Russia with the recording, life and future for totalitarianism would have its throat cut. But quick. There would be no dallying. As everyone now realized, there had been too much patience already.

"Monk," Doc said.

Monk jumped nervously. "Yeah?"

"You're working according to plan, aren't you?" Doc asked. "In other words, you're headed for a spot where you have a shortwave radio transmitter concealed?"

"That's right."

"I'm uneasy about that," Doc said frankly. "There has been a leak somewhere. The way that girl Seryi stepped into the picture . . . Mahli's phone call to get you away from the meeting place so the girl could contact us . . . and the way she was taken out of our hands later—all that had a quality about it of being rigged."

"I don't see where the hell the leak could have been," Monk muttered. "God knows, Ham and I have been so careful we fooled ourselves."

"How do you explain this Seryi?"

"The same way you do—a counterplot of some kind." Monk squirmed uncomfortably. "But what kind? What's the rig?"

"Apparently we aren't being followed. We weren't molested at Frunzoff's place, although the girl herself gave us the address."

"Blazes! You think they may know about the radio station and be laying for us there?"

"Why not? If they knew as much as they did, they could know about the radio."

"Doc, we've *got* to get to a radio transmitter. Otherwise we're behind the eight ball. Touching off the rest of our plan depends on that."

"Turn north at the next corner," Doc said abruptly. "We're going to raid a Soviet shortwave station and use that."

On the Kashira road, a few miles south of the Moscow city environs, they turned off the main thoroughfare and parked at the foot of a hill on which stood a group of radio towers.

"We've got to do this quick and clean," Doc warned. "We'll try it the way we got to Frunzoff."

"Wonder how many engineers will be on duty," Ham said uneasily.

"Two, according to the information I have."

Ham glanced at the big bronze man in surprise. "You mean you dug up information like that ahead of time?"

Doc shrugged. "It wasn't hard to get. The consulate obtained it—remember the fuss that was kicked up recently about Soviet radio jamming our own propaganda broadcasts? The Communists denied it, of course, and made a big show of naming and identifying all their radio stations—actually revealing about half of them, probably. Anyway, we got enough information from that."

They worked through the darkness, sleet making walking difficult. The steepness of the path did not help. They came presently to a drab block of a concrete building with lighted windows with a big *Octopozho!* warning sign about high voltages.

Doc wheeled suddenly, said, "Listen!"

Startled, Monk stiffened so abruptly that his

feet slipped on the ice and he fell. He did not fall heavily, and remained as he landed, supported on his braced hands.

In the night there was nothing that seemed abnormal. Only the humming of a transformer inside the building, the glassy creaking of sleet on tree twigs.

"I believe I heard a car stop down there on the road," Doc said uneasily. "I'm not sure. . . . We can't take a chance, though. Monk, you'd better check on it. And be careful."

"Nobody could have followed us," Monk muttered. "And nobody knew we were coming here. We didn't know it ourselves an hour ago."

"Be careful anyway," Doc warned.

Monk grunted. "You want me to wait at our car, if it's a false alarm?" He turned and began retracing the route downhill. He went with care, keeping in the very darkest places, and listening frequently. He had barked the knuckles of his left hand when he fell a moment ago, and he twisted bits of ice off a branch that whacked him in the face, and held the ice against the raw areas.

Having heard nothing and seen nothing alarming, Monk reached the vicinity of their car. Now he went with great care, a step at a time, although he was convinced that Doc Savage had made one of his rare errors. A car had stopped on the road? Hell, what if it had? Anybody driving a night like this would be stopping often to whittle ice off his windshield. It was inconceivable that anyone had trailed them. . . .

Monk suddenly grew colder than even the chilly

night warranted. His mouth felt very dry. Still, he had heard and seen nothing. But he didn't like the idea that had just hit him.

He moved forward a step at a time, now with a gun in his hand. The car had become something to be feared and avoided—but he had to learn whether he was right. He found the right-hand door, opened it warily, felt inside, and located the tiny portable two-way radio which he had kept in his possession on the chance that its necessity would outweigh the almost certain fact that the fancy Soviet monitoring system would spot any bootleg transmitter a couple of moments after it went on the air.

Monk turned on the receiver. He could check what he wanted to check with the receiver alone. He advanced the gain only enough to register the tube hiss, then began running the tuning mechanism through all the frequencies it would tune. When he got into the very-high-frequency end of the spectrum, it began to "block."

His blood chilled. Receivers would "block" in this fashion only when a transmitter was so very close that its immediate field paralyzed the vacuum tubes.

He tried to swallow. *Monk, you fool, you've been suckered with a trick you've used yourself a dozen times!* There was a shortwave transmitter attached somewhere to the car. It needn't be large; a case the size of a couple of cigarette packages might contain it. And it could be traced easily with almost any sort of loop or beam directional antennae.

Doc had been right, then. There had been a car on the road, and it had been following them through the medium of radio. *My God, where can that transmitter be hidden? How long has it been there? Who put it there?*

That line of thought iced up completely when he felt metal against the back of his neck.

"*Khto tam?*" a voice said unpleasantly, and reworded the inquiry in English. "Who is this?"

"Use that gun on him," another voice said sharply, and Monk had the absurd and ghastly feeling that he had gone far out somewhere in a black endless space that was flecked faintly with crimson; there was no impression of falling or even of motion, but everything was perfectly static and as restful as death. There was the added disagreeable fact that he didn't seem to have his head with him.

7

Inside the radio-transmitter room, Doc Savage stood frowning down at a turntable on which a record was being broadcast. It was a propaganda piece, optimistically beamed at the United States in English, and so unbelievable that it wouldn't be convincing. The same thing had happened to the Nazis when they started believing the sound of their own voices.

Ham Brooks said, "We won't have to change the beam setting for direction. The indicator says approximately due north, and there's enough spread to hit the monitors which will be listening for us."

Doc crossed over and swung out the transmitter rack cover and examined the oscillator section where the frequency was first created which would later go out on the ether in the form of radio transmission. It was here that he would have to change the wavelength of the transmitted signal so that the monitor stations in America would get it immediately.

The transmitter, he knew, was a copy of an American rig, even to the shape of the crystal holder. The crystal controlled the wavelength.

"You mean you came prepared with a spare crystal cut to our American monitoring frequency?" Ham exploded.

"It seemed like a good idea," Doc said. "Here we go. That telephone is going to ring the minute we go off the air. Answer and tell them it's transmitter trouble."

He pulled switches, got the outfit off the air, yanked the crystal, substituted his own, did a quick job of retuning, picked up a microphone, and adjusted the gain on it.

Ham's jaw fell when he heard the coded message Doc spoke into the mike. It was spoken in Russian, cleverly done, consisting of a berating tirade directed against the engineer in the station. It was something that would pass as a row which two engineers were having over an electrical difficulty with the equipment. Something that a live microphone might have happened to pick up.

Doc finished, jerked the station off the air, changed the crystals back the way they were, and began retuning again. The telephone rang. Ham picked up the instrument, listened, said angrily in Russian, *"Eta ochen groosna!"* He was evidently shouted at, because he shouted back, this time without an apology. He ended with a tirade, tore the phone loose from its wires, and said, "I hope these engineers had a reputation for bad tempers."

"The station is back on the air," Doc said. He went over and broke a restorative ampul under the nostrils of each of the two Russian station engineers, ensuring their awakening within a few moments. "Let's get out of here."

"How long have we got to wait?" Ham asked.

"Four or five hours," Doc guessed. "That is based on the weather, though. If everything is grounded, it might be more difficult."

"These sleet storms usually break up a little after daylight, don't they?"

"Let's hope this one does."

The girl Seryi stood in the darkness, a tall cold figure in a sheath of a black raincoat on which the ice clung.

She spoke two English words and one Russian one: "You understand *roozhyo?*" She also moved her hand a little to make sure they saw the dark gun there.

Doc Savage stared at her blankly, thinking how silly it was that she would ask them if they understood a gun, phrasing it that way. Then he realized she was probably very terrified, even if more determined than terrified, and to be dealt with cautiously.

"I waited here in your car," she said. "It will hold three, will it not? I wish to ride back to the city with you."

Ham Brooks said, "Oh, brother!" softly, and then on a wild note demanded, "Where's Monk—?" He changed that hurriedly to, "Where's that monkey-faced commissar?"

"That is why I wish to ride with you." Seryi's voice was as loose as a leaf in the darkness.

"Huh?"

"I am instructed to tell you," Seryi said, "that the commissar—shouldn't we call him Mr. Monk Mayfair, eminent chemist, adventurer, and Doc Savage associate—has exactly two hours to live unless you rescue him."

"How come?"

"Hold it a minute," Doc Savage said. He had

been trying to figure out how they had been
trailed here, and he'd gotten the same thought
Monk had investigated. Doc switched on the shortwave radio, tuned the higher frequencies, and got
the telltale receiver blocking. He investigated.

The transmitter was in a cardboard box that
was properly marked *Vnootrennyaya troopka.*
Inner tube. Doc tore it open and stopped transmission. He went back and confronted the girl.

"All right," he said. "We have been outsmarted.
Your outfit trailed us here, and grabbed Monk.
Now what?"

"Two hours isn't much," Seryi said nervously.
"You'd better get moving."

Without a word, Doc put the car in motion.
He backed and turned carefully, and on the ice-
glazed highway he headed toward Moscow. The
wheel chains made a monotonous whining, but
the sleet did not seem to be falling as heavily.
The girl's voice began to come, a thin sound of
fright driven through defiance, from the darkness
within the rear seat.

"Here it is," she said. "Wherever there is an
organization with people in it, and some have
power and some haven't, there is continual scheming and maneuvering by those who are not at the
top and want to climb there."

Doc said, "Is she holding that gun on you, Ham?"

"She's holding it on you," Ham said. "She's
keeping it pointed at the middle of your back."

"All right. I wanted to know. Go ahead, Miss
Seryi. If that's your name."

"It's Seryi Mitroff," she said bitterly. "As I
started to say, where there is power, there is invariably hunger for that power—"

"Skip that part about human greed," Doc said. "What you're saying is that in politics there are two groups. Those in. And the outs. Which are you?"

She hesitated, then said curtly, "I'm an out."

"And you're working with a group of outs?"

"Yes."

"And you want in?"

"Naturally," she said.

Doc Savage swung the car abruptly, turning into a side road which, according to the maps he had memorized before starting the project, circled through a village named Tormas, then entered Moscow by a route that would put them on Twerskaja Street when they approached Red Square, which was the heart of the city.

"You aren't being followed!" Seryi said.

"Not if we can help it," Doc agreed. "You don't mind our taking a less obvious route into the city? After all, we've made one fool move tonight."

"You weren't so foolish." Seryi hesitated, and then added with a little pride, "We have in our group about ten men who are as skilled espionage agents as any in the Soviet, which I imagine makes them the best in the world. Those ten have been working on this with all their wiles, and they haven't found out too much."

"They certainly learned too much to suit us," Doc told her wryly.

"No. We're quite puzzled."

"You learned Monk and Ham were my associates."

"Not until tonight. All we had been able to ascertain was that they were up to something—

and they were looking for the mystery man of the Soviet. Frunzoff."

"How did you know it was Frunzoff?"

"Who else could it be? Or was it Frunzoff? That's what we want to find out, for one thing."

Her voice had become sharply eager in the back seat, and Doc noted the excitement, speculated about it a moment, and then said, "It was a clever idea, Miss Mitroff. You didn't exaggerate when you said your associates were experts at espionage."

Ham demanded explosively, "Doc! Doc, I don't think they *knew* that Frunzoff was the spider who held all the webs!"

"That's what I mean. They're trying to use us to confirm that fact. That's why they furnished us with Frunzoff's address."

"Damn! We haven't been half-smart."

Seryi Mitroff remarked wryly, "You think not? You might ask Mahli. Mahli is one of the greatest undercover agents who ever lived. Just to show you how great he is, I'll tell you this: he has been personally decorated by Stalin five times." She hesitated when Ham Brooks laughed, then demanded angrily, "What is funny?"

Ham told her, "You sound like the people with the swastikas on their arms sounded a few years ago when they spoke of the paperhanger. Remember Adolf? He handed out a few decorations in his time, but looking back now, they didn't mean much, did they?"

"Go ahead and insult me," Seryi snapped. "I was paying you a compliment—Mahli knows skill, and he was vastly impressed by your performance. Of course, he didn't know that you were associates of the fabulous Doc Savage. He only knew you were clever espionage men on a job, and that you were seeking Frunzoff."

"You mean," Ham asked in astonishment, "you didn't know Frunzoff was the all-important one until you saw we were trying to find him?"

"That's about it," she confessed. "You can see why we were impressed. You had come into Russia, two foreigners, and you dug up something we had only suspected was true, and moreover, you learned the man's identity."

"You're impressed?" Ham asked dryly.

"Certainly."

"I'm not," Ham said. "Right now, I can't think of a job where Monk and I made more fool moves and got in a worse mess."

Doc asked, "What is your proposition, young lady?"

"Tell us what you found out from Frunzoff, and give us the proof you took—the kind of information you got from Frunzoff would be so startling that you would have to prove its authenticity—and that is all we want."

"And the price you offer?"

"The return of your man Monk Mayfair, alive."

"And an unhindered escape from Russia, I presume?"

"Naturally. We could help you escape, if you wish. But presumably you have a better plan for flight than we could concoct."

"Just what," Doc asked, "do you intend to do with this information which you seem to imagine we got from Frunzoff?"

"You got it, all right," she said.

"How do you know?"

"You went to his house, didn't you? And then

71

headed for a radio station. Oh, you got what you came after, all right."

"What," said Doc, "do you think you would do with this plum you feel we picked?"

She laughed grimly.

"How long," she asked, "do you think Frunzoff would last if the Central Committee knew three foreign agents had calmly walked in and milked him of all they wanted to know?"

"My impression," Doc said, "is that the Central Committee doesn't know Frunzoff exists as anyone of importance."

The girl started to say something, stammered, and fell silent.

"To put it more correctly," Doc suggested, "if the Central Committee can be shown Stalin has prepared such a secret ace as Frunzoff, Stalin's hold will be weakened. The idea is to tear down Stalin. Right?"

"I don't see why you should object to that," she snapped.

Doc said in a conversational tone, "I can't think of a very sound reason, either. Ham, is she still holding the gun on me?"

"She keeps the gun pointed right at your back," Ham said.

"At the middle of my back?"

"Yes. The bullets would go through the seat, of course."

"Take the gun away from her," Doc said.

Ham must have worked very fast. Doc was set for the shock of the bullet—not that he quite lacked confidence in the bulletproof chain-mesh undergarment he was wearing, but the idea of stopping a bullet wasn't reassuring. When the gun exploded, which it did twice, the slugs drove through the side of the car. He heard the gun fall to the floor. But that didn't settle it; a series of sounds of violent motion followed, then a long, painful yodellike expression of pain from Ham Brooks.

Doc stopped the car, which was not moving fast. He turned in the seat, and as nearly as he could determine in the darkness, Ham was getting the worst of it. Doc, amazed, joined the struggle with some caution. The caution was justified, because the forefinger of his right hand got a quick disjointing, he narrowly missed losing an eye, and his neck got a painful wrench. All of that in about two and a half seconds, before he subdued the girl.

There was a period of silence in the little car.

"Whew!" Ham said weakly. "Don't ever, whatever you do, let Monk hear that a slip of a girl practically took me apart and threw the pieces away."

"Are you badly hurt?" Doc demanded.

"Of course I'm hurt!" Ham yelled. "I'm hurt all over. My God, this babe knows judo tricks I never heard of."

"If you'll hold her," Doc said, "I'll get the truth serum ready."

"Do I have to?" Ham asked gingerly. "All right. I'll try to hold her. But be ready to rescue me if she as much as gets one finger loose."

Doc found the gun and tossed it out of the car. Then he gripped his disjointed finger, wrenched it back into normalcy, and felt gingerly of his aching neck. He got out the equipment case that held the truth serum and its necessary apparatus.

73

"Let me have her wrist," he said.

Seryi Mitroff made a completely cold-blooded comment. "So that is how you got to Frunzoff," she said.

8

Mahli, the great oaf of a man, finished explaining
the situation to Monk Mayfair, speaking English
so naturally that Monk could have imagined, had
he not been too frightened to imagine anything,
that he was listening to a salesman try to sell him
an insurance policy in New York. Mahli was
clearly one of the very few men whom Monk had
met whose looks were more deceiving than his
own. Mahli had the build and appearance of a
hooligan of the most stupid type. By now, though,
there wasn't any doubt in Monk's mind about the
man being educated, clever, and probably as
warmhearted as a blackjack.

"You understand?" Mahli asked.

"I guess so," Monk muttered. "I'm your down
payment on the information you imagine we got
from Frunzoff."

"Exactly."

"It's all right if I don't feel happy about it,
isn't it?" Monk asked bitterly.

"You're physically intact. You should feel somewhat fortunate about that."

"And about this knot on my head, I suppose?
Presumably this lightning that keeps striking me
is coming from some sort of protuberance? Do you
mind if I feel and find out?"

"Sit still."

"Okay."

"Sit very still," Mahli warned. "It has finally dawned on us that you are a Doc Savage associate. That, if you don't mind my saying so, will persuade us to shoot you instantly if you as much as sneeze."

"Okay. I had gathered that."

"Good."

"Where are we?" Monk asked.

"No answer to that," Mahli said.

Monk glanced around, being careful not even to move his eyes too abruptly because he didn't doubt in the least that he would be shot if his captors became alarmed. Not that they weren't alarmed already; they just weren't at the point of disposing of him. Monk felt they wished to do so. He had never seen a group of men who were more convinced they had caught a Tartar. Doc Savage's reputation, Monk reflected, could be quite a liability.

He saw a grimy cavern of a room furnished with three iron cots, some bedclothing, a coal stove, a table, two chairs, and not much else, if one omitted the odor of too much unwashed occupancy. Someone's living quarters, presumably.

"There are seven men guarding you," Mahli warned suddenly and hoarsely. "You haven't a chance to escape."

"Take it easy," Monk said. "You're so nervous you're getting me upset."

"No chance for you in flight, understand! There is myself and seven very good men. There is the Russian Security Police, the OGPU, the NKVD, the VSNK—"

"We have a little of that alphabet soup back home," Monk said. "Is here where it started?"

"You mustn't try to escape."

"Oh, mustn't I?"

Mahli scowled, then muttered, "It would be a relief if you would promise not to try. Would you give your word?"

Monk laughed in his face. "Sure. I'll promise—that it won't be a try. It'll be a success, brother. You won't know what's happened until it's *sleeshkam pozna*, comrade. Too late." Monk hesitated, eyed the big man, and added, "Why the outsized tizzy, large *tovarich*? I don't make you as a guy who gets that scared of me."

"Much is at stake," Mahli said frankly.

"Yeah?"

"I will speak straight words, ugly one. It has long been suspected that Stalin has groomed a faceless one to step into his shoes. It would be a relief to many if that one were eliminated."

"A relief to the other candidates," Monk said. "I see what you mean."

"If Stalin has prepared this faceless one, it will make him no friends."

Monk nodded. "Among the other candidates. I can see that, too."

"Is Frunzoff such a faceless one? And did you get proof tonight?"

Monk grinned. "What was it you said awhile ago? 'No answer to that'? That's me all over, *tovarich*. You're speaking to a fencepost."

Beside the grimy window a man cursed impatiently. They listened, and there was the sound of a man singing in the distance, loudly and happily. The aria was a Tchaikovsky bit, and the singer applied Russian words, then switched over into another tongue that was certainly not Russian. There were but a few words of this, then he swung back into Russian. "A noisy fool for so early in the morning," muttered the man who had sworn.

Monk leaned back, trying to look relaxed. It was Doc Savage out there, and the language that was not Russian was ancient Mayan, understood by very few in the so-called civilized world outside of Doc Savage and his aides.

The information Doc had inserted in the song was a little upsetting. They were out of anesthetic gas, Doc said. Any help Monk got would be the hard way.

Monk placed his feet on the floor so that he could get a quick start, made a mental notation that he would like very much to be safe in New York, then waited. That was about all he could do. That, and hope it wouldn't be too long, which it wasn't.

The fire began in an alleylike court at the rear. Monk, because he was expecting something, saw the smoke first, and had difficulty keeping from pointing it out. Then a man yelled, pointed. There was, as might be expected, a rush for the window. What was burning down in the alley, they never found out, and it was the least of what happened anyway.

The window went first. Sash, glass, everything, it came to pieces, letting in a sheet of bluish flame, a gulp of driven air, and an incredible amount of noise. Monk understood fully that it was a small explosive grenade, applied to the window for a distraction. He was surprised, though, when Doc Savage came in through the window after it.

Monk was on his feet and after the guard at the door by now. The guard, the only man at the door, had been bounced back against the panel by the explosion—by the surprise of it rather than the force—and had half-turned and was fending off with one arm and fumbling for a gun with the other. Monk did his best to put his right fist entirely through the man's middle, and when the fellow doubled, used his right fist to change the shape of the man's jaw considerably.

He knew by now that Doc must be in the room. There was quite a bit of smoke, but enough was added to the activity to indicate Doc. The building was an old-fashioned stone affair with ledges outside the window, so he imagined Doc had stepped in from next door.

Monk turned, picked up a chair, and made for Mahli. The latter was on his knees, fumbling for a gun that he must have dropped in the excitement.

Doc said in Mayan, "Get going, Monk. Never mind cracking heads."

Monk hesitated, thought of the beating he'd taken in the night near the radio station, and threw the chair at Mahli. It didn't damage Mahli much. Monk started for the big Russian, but Doc said more sharply, "Cut it out! Get going."

Ham Brooks was outside the door. He said, "You took long enough getting out of there," to Monk, and they ran down a passage, then downstairs.

The night outside was turning into a shiny ugly dawn that made their faces look a little more red and harried than they were.

"Where is this good-looking Seryi babe I've been hearing about?" Monk asked. He was not puffing noticeably.

"Tied up in the back of the car," Ham said.

They came to the little Russian copy of a German motorcar. Monk piled into the rear, then asked, "In the back of what car?"

Doc, on an impressive note of disgust, said, "She's gone, you mean?"

"Then so will the car keys be, and probably the ignition wiring too," Ham predicted.

He was wrong, though.

They drove hard and deviously for about one *verst*, the Russian equivalent of two-thirds of a mile, then traveled decorously. Reaching the wide Twerskoj Boulevard, Doc reached down to tinker with the radio receiver and get it on the Moscow police frequency. Mostly he tuned in electrical interference from the tramway cars which, even at this ungodly hour, were packed with work-bound people.

"How about briefing me on what happened?" Monk asked. Ham did so, finishing, "That Seryi turned out to be about the poorest example of truth-serum efficiency we ever saw. But we did get it out of her that you were being held at that address."

"And you left her tied up in the backseat?" Monk inquired.

"Why not? By all normal standards, she would

have been woozy from the truth serum for an hour longer."

"Who tied her up?" Monk asked.

"I did," Doc said uncomfortably. "And let's not go into that."

Monk noted the swollen finger which Seryi had unjointed for Doc earlier. "That's a bad-looking finger you've got. What happened to it?" Monk remarked.

Doc drove intently and said nothing.

Monk turned to Ham and asked, "You blacked your eye, shyster? Or did you know you've got a very outstanding shiner?"

Ham winced. "There was a little fight a minute ago. Or didn't you happen to notice?"

"I thought it took half an hour or so for an eye to get black after the punch," Monk said dryly. "What have you developed? A quick color change?"

Ham hastily changed his explanation to, "I guess I got an eye bruised when I slipped on the ice back at the radio station. Sure, I recall it now."

Monk expressed his disbelief with a snort.

"You boys are tearing down my yen to meet this Seryi," he said.

"I do hope you meet her," Ham snapped.

"Yeah?"

"Nothing would give me quite as much satisfaction," Ham assured him disagreeably.

9

Beyond the picturesque iron bridge over the Moskwa River near the southeast Kremlin wall, they turned into a side street, parked, left the car, and walked four blocks over the glazed pavement to a small private garage where Monk and Ham had a change of cars waiting. This one was a light U.S. Army command car which had been converted with a coat of paint and a brand plate giving the false impression that it was Soviet-made.

"The airport now?" Ham asked.

Doc Savage consulted his watch, then nodded. "Yes. About the right amount of time has elapsed."

"Provided," Ham said, "the American monitors picked up our radio message."

Monk shuddered. "Don't be pessimistic. Smile at fate and keep her happy."

Ham was tuning the radio to the Soviet police wavelength again. "You been listening to the local cops?" he demanded. "If not, just fan out your ears. They're not passing up that mess we just made of Mahli and his friends." Ham pointed at the radio. "Go ahead. Listen. Then be an optimist."

What they were hearing was the Moscow police spreading a dragnet. There was a grim efficiency about it. And to complicate matters, the police had a general description of them—they were pictured as three men, one a giant, one an apish fellow, and one *kraseevyi*. Monk grimaced when he heard the Russian word describing Ham. Ham chuckled. "That's me. Handsome," he said.

The radio was an all-wave model, and Doc indicated it impatiently, saying, "Never mind amusing yourselves listening to the police uproar. Tune in on the Soviet Air Traffic Control frequency, and let's see if we're going to stand a chance of getting out of this."

The SATC wavelength was disturbingly quiet when they got the radio set up on it. They drove in silence, listening. Doc's face began to get a metallic angularity that meant strain. Ham and Monk stared at their watches uneasily.

They had driven about ten *verstahs*. Outside, the sleet no longer fell, the windshield being clear except for the condensation on the inner surface, which Doc kept scrubbing away with a palm. There was a cold wind that blew hard and tumbled dark sheeplike clouds and occasionally nudged the car insolently.

Suddenly the Soviet Air Traffic Control came to life, spluttering and astonished. An American transport plane was scheduled for early arrival at the Moscow airport. There was some confusion about clearance for the ship. Soviet Army Air Force Interceptor broke into the communications channel with the pointed information that the plane was going to be shot down. That added quite a lot to the uproar. Air Force Interception was informed the plane had special diplomatic clearance.

Interception wished to know—in about those words—how the blue hell that had happened. They were informed that the answer was simple enough for even Interception to get through its thick head —a very important American was on the plane. An American that had enough weight internationally that instantaneous clearance had been arranged. Who would that imperialistic so-and-so be? Interception wished to know.

Doc Savage. Doc Savage was aboard the plane. It seemed that last night a demonstration of radar-blocking by rocket in the American zone of Germany had gone wrong, and the rocket had mistracked and probably landed somewhere in Soviet territory. The experiment had been conducted by two of Doc Savage's aides, Renny Renwick and electrical wizard Long Tom Roberts. They were testing a device on which Doc Savage had assisted in development.

Doc Savage was flying to Moscow to personally demand the return of his radar-blocking gadget that had strayed. With him were two of his aides, Monk Mayfair and Ham Brooks.

Monk grinned at Ham.

"So you're twins," he remarked. "As the fellow says, 'What a revoltin' development that is.'"

With the Moscow airport hangars bulking on their left, Doc Savage swung the car around to the rear of the Comrade Soldiers' Club, a large drab wooden building with the single word *Eentendahnstva* across the front. There were other cars there, and a couple of trucks.

"You fellows are familiar with the procedure we hope to follow?" Doc asked.

Monk nodded. "I should be. I've repeated it to myself every night since I've been in Russia.

Sort of a part of my nightly prayer." He glanced at Ham. "Cripes, have you gone back to carrying that cane?"

Ham Brooks, for as long as Monk had known him, had invariably carried a slender black sword-cane. The cane had rarely been out of Ham's hand, and it was almost a part of him, and certainly a part of his character. During the time they had been in Soviet territory, Ham had naturally forsaken his trademark.

Monk pointed at the cane Ham had extracted from the car trunk. "That's not yours. It's not even the type you would carry. Where'd you swipe it?"

"Come on, stupid," Ham said.

The cane was a heavy knurled article of iron-wood with inlaid bands of gold and silver—platinum, Monk decided, taking a closer look and revising his opinion—and it bore no resemblance whatever to Ham's neat dark sword-cane. It looked valuable, though. And useful in a skull-breaking contest.

They crossed a cobbled road, passed between two buildings, and Doc stopped at a narrow door. He tapped on the door. Three raps, a pause, two, a pause, then three more rappings. They waited. The building eaves were heavy with icicles, and one of these broke loose and fell, causing Monk to jump, literally, out of one shoe. He bent over, grumbling and embarrassed, and was stamping his foot into the shoe when the door opened.

A man came out of the door. A sullen-faced man in workman's clothing. He muttered the Russian good morning, "*Dobraye ootra,*" without any visible pleasure whatever, and stalked past them. If they meant anything to him, it certainly wasn't evident.

"I remember that chap," Ham said with pleasure. "The last time I saw him, he was a prince of the Imperial Japanese family in Tokyo, about a year after Pearl Harbor."

Doc said, "We're to wait inside. It seems to be going according to schedule."

The room which they entered was a naked place without furniture, but with three nails driven into one wall. From the three nails were suspended clothes hangers with three suits, shirts, neckties, to fit them. Socks and shoes were ready on the floor.

Monk's necktie was a terrific yellow. He eyed it with pleasure.

Moscow zone Traffic Control kept the American transport plane circling the airport for half an hour by claiming there was a stack of air traffic in the overcast, which was a lie. The object of the discourtesy, uniquely enough, was not characteristic nastiness, but an effort to delay the ship's arrival until a Russian dignitary named Zardnov reached the field.

Zardnov—his full name was Oldenny Zardnov —was currently an acting delegate to the United Nations. This meant that he functioned at Lake Success when Molotov and Gromyko were absent, and it also indicated that Zardnov was currently in favor. That made him an important man. Regardless of the Russian obstruction attitude in the UN, they had certainly assigned their top men to the sessions. So Zardnov was prominent. He was currently in Moscow for instructions.

Zardnov reached the airport with his face still puffed from sleep, and his temper bad. He was a stocky man of about Molotov's build, but with thicker lips and large damp eyes. Indicative of his status, he was accompanied by four bodyguards and two secretaries in two other cars.

It was inevitable that Zardnov would be called to deal with Doc Savage's descent on Moscow. Zardnov stared upward angrily, although the plane was too high in the overcast to be heard. He had made a violent speech at Lake Success concerning Doc Savage, branding the bronze man a charlatan and a troublemaker, and had been laughed off the floor for his pains.

"Let the ship land," Zardnov said grimly. "I will make this Doc Savage a speech before we send him back without his silly rocket. It will be a satisfaction." He turned to a secretary. "Has the rocket been found?"

"There is a great search, and it will be found," said the lackey cautiously.

The plane broke through the overcast at fourteen hundred, and it made an impressive sight approaching the field. It was a six-jet ship with V-wings and a probable airspeed top of well beyond five hundred. It came in hot, gear down, touched the runway, and presently taxied along the strip to a tired brick building that was a former administration building, now unused since the construction of the new terminal in which Zardnov waited.

"Tell them to come here! Here!" Zardnov yelled.

The control tower conveyed the information to the Yank pilot, who informed the tower that an American embassy attaché was waiting at the old terminal to greet Doc Savage, and that was where they were going. The hell with Mr. Zardnov.

Zardnov got the point. He raised his cane on high and shook it. The cane was quite a hefty one of ironwood with gold and platinum inlay, and carrying it was not an affectation with Zardnov. He needed it. During the early days of red terror, two days following August 30, 1918, when a girl named Kaplan shot Lenin as he left a workers' meeting in Moscow, Zardnov had himself received a bullet in the knee, which had left a permanent disablement. The knee was inclined at the most unexpected moments to fold and deposit Zardnov on the floor if he didn't have the cane for quick support. Consequently he was never without it.

The car whisked Zardnov to the old terminal, and he saw with some satisfaction that political police had surrounded Doc Savage, Monk Mayfair, and Ham Brooks the instant they stepped from the plane.

Zardnov saw with a touch of disgust that American embassy attaché Clyde Warper had forced his way through and joined the plane arrivals. The disgust wasn't for Clyde Warper personally. It was just that diplomats had an understanding, a gentleman's agreement, that each fellow's country wouldn't abuse the other's diplomats. The diplomatic gentlemen might plot wars and casually arrange the slaughter of a few million civilians, but they mustn't have their hair mussed. That was the deal from time immemorial, and Zardnov certainly wasn't going to break up the play, being a fellow who needed diplomatic immunity more than anyone else.

Clyde Warper had whisked the arrivals into a room in the old terminal before Zardnov could join them. That was all right; the political police were on the job.

Warper and Zardnov were as polite as two cats climbing out of a cream jar. Clyde Warper introduced Doc Savage, Monk Mayfair, and Ham Brooks.

Zardnov leaned on his cane and scowled. He had not personally met Doc Savage or his aides previously. He was interested in the group.

The big bronze man was carrying a metal equipment case, and as he began telling Zardnov the purpose of his visit to Moscow—it concerned the incident of the runaway rocket last night, the way he told it—he gestured with emphasis with the hand holding the case. The case lid flew open, apparently by accident, and a number of objects fell out. One of these burst with about the commotion of a ripe egg, and an incredible quantity of black smoke exuded from it.

In a couple of seconds the inside of the room was as black as the interior of a goat.

"It's harmless! It's harmless!" Doc Savage was shouting. "It's merely a smoke grenade. Quite harmless. Stand where you are, everyone. Somebody open the window."

Nobody seemed to be doing much standing still. Feet were whetting the floor excitedly.

The cane which was supporting Zardnov was jerked from under him, and he sat down heavily on the floor. The cane left his fingers somehow.

The room rang with Russian profanity.

Someone opened the window. Smoke came out.

In the American plane, the crew members saw

the smoke, heard the excitement, and they left the ship and bolted in a body for the administration building to learn what was happening and offer whatever aid seemed appropriate.

The smoke exuded from the window rapidly, the air in the room cleared, and so did the excitement.

Zardnov discovered a uniformed Russian policeman standing beside him holding his, Zardnov's, prized cane. "Did you jerk that from under me, you fool?" Zardnov snarled.

The Soviet cop became as white as a Siberian winter, probably not without reason. "Oh, no, sir! It was pushed into my hand. Someone thrust it upon me in the blackness!" he blurted.

The crewmen of the American ship returned to their craft, at the pointed suggestion of the police. It seemed they didn't have clearance to leave their ship, a technicality newly devised for the embarrassment of individuals the Communists wished to embarrass.

Not unnaturally, considering the excitement, no one happened to notice that three more men returned to the plane than had left it to investigate the uproar. Three. A large man, a short wide one, and a slender one. Other than this physical similarity, however, they bore no great resemblance to Doc Savage and his two aides.

In the old terminal, Doc Savage was apologizing for his carelessness.

From apologies, Doc shifted to a stiff demand that he be given custody of the remains of the radar-blocking rocket which had strayed. He intimated there was great likelihood that the Soviets had found the lost rocket by now. Hadn't

they had representatives at the scene of the rocket
firing in the American zone last night? There was
an intimation that Doc thought the Soviets weren't
above tampering with the rocket to cause the
accident.

Zardnov's argument took the line that this was
a petty matter, and under the jurisdiction of
another department anyway. He, Zardnov, was
powerless, as a matter of fact. This, of course, was
a colossal lie, but Zardnov enjoyed telling it.

The argument grew heated. This didn't mean
the language was profane, although the meanings
inherent in the words were more blistering than
a mule skinner's vocabulary.

Zardnov said he would do Doc Savage a great
favor and telephone the Central Executive in
Charge of Finding Lost Rockets. He did go to a
telephone, and called his wife to learn whether
she was still being unreasonable about the
Kronstadt girl with whom Zardnov was living part-
time. She was. Not bothered much, Zardnov
returned to Doc Savage.

"I am informed there will be a full investigation
concerning the rocket, and a decision reached. That
will take about ten days. You will be informed,"
Zardnov said without batting an eye. "I am very
sorry."

Doc protested vociferously. He noted Monk and
Ham watching him impatiently. The switch with
the three ringers from the plane had been managed
deftly during the experience with the smoke
grenade. Through the window, Doc had seen the
ringers board the ship. They were safe. The ship's
documents numbered them among the crew, in
case there was any doubt in Russian minds.

Nothing remained, then, but to wait to be ordered out of Russia, which Doc imagined would not be long coming.

The switch at the airport, quite an elaborate bit of chicanery, had two objectives—to make it seem that Doc, Monk, and Ham had been on the plane and could not have been in Moscow that night, and to draw attention to the matter so that when it was publicized later, it would be believable. The first was a temporary blindfold for the Russians; the second would be a headache for them later, if things went well.

Zardnov was grinning.

"I have also other news for you," he said in his poor English. "Your permission to visit Russia has been canceled. You will, unfortunately, have to leave immediately."

That was what Doc had been awaiting, but he made a loud objection.

"You will have to leave," Zardnov insisted.

Doc glanced at Monk and Ham, and to their relief, shrugged. "There'll be plenty of hell raised about this," he assured Zardnov.

They prepared to leave. The man from the consulate, Clyde Warper, registered his formal opinion. Outside, the plane skipper signaled, and the crew began getting into position.

A Russian arrived with a wild look and grabbed Zardnov's shoulder. Zardnov, the man said, was wanted on the telephone. Looking surprised and uneasy, Zardnov turned and hurried toward a booth.

"I don't like the looks of this," Doc said grimly. "Let's get out of here."

They had almost reached the door when Zardnov

screamed; the high piping sound of the man's voice went running through the building like raw little animals.

"Seize them!" he shrieked. "They mustn't escape! They have . . ." He apparently realized he didn't know what they had done. "That was the Kremlin itself on the telephone!" he croaked.

Doc Savage, lunging through the door, found himself looking down the muzzles of half a dozen guns, and more weapons were joining the battery.

"Hold them!" Zardnov was bellowing excitedly. "The Kremlin wants them."

10

They could see, beyond the window with its lacing of steel bars, the pale pink brick wall of the Kremlin with its battlements and citadellike towers. It was very cold; the sleet gave the outer world a shiny effect, and a few thin hard snow pellets were traveling in the air like frightened gnats.

The room where they waited was of stone and bare, hard, ancient *doop* wood and as naked as they were. Their clothing had been taken. They were still dripping from the violent shower bath they had been forced to take.

Somewhere in the ineffectual daylight outside, a peal of bells began. The sound came from the tower above the Spasskiye Vorota, the Gate of Salvation, that an Englishman had built in the fifteenth century. The bells pealed the "Internationale," which meant that it was noon. The "Internationale" was played at twelve and six o'clock, and at three and nine o'clock the Russian Revolutionary Funeral March was on the repertoire.

"Twelve o'clock," Doc remarked.

"Damn, I'm cold," Monk complained.

"Think about the firing squad," Ham advised him. "That should warm you up."

"You believe they'll do that to us?" Monk asked in alarm.

"Why not?" Ham said bitterly. "After all, we—"

"—are perfectly innocent," Doc interjected warningly. He added in Mayan, "There seems to be no hidden microphone, which probably means there is one." In English he continued, "This is an outrage. Our diplomatic immunity as military emissaries has been violated. Such a thing is unheard of, even here."

The door opened, armed guards entered, and they were told harshly, "*Syoodah!*" The march carried them down a corridor past an almost continuous array of armed men who eyed their nakedness with ugly pleasure.

The destination proved to be the X-ray room of the Kremlin hospital, where they were X-rayed in rapid succession from head to toe.

"What's the idea of this shenanigan?" Monk pondered angrily. "They trying to identify us by our dental work or by my flat feet?"

"A further search for secret weapons, probably," Doc guessed.

Ham contributed, "Or maybe they think we swallowed the keys to the city."

The X-raying completed, their skin was subjected to inspection with infrared and ultraviolet light, clearly a search for secret writing. Their fingernails were examined, scraped; their hair was combed and the combings passed on to a laboratory. "This is getting preposterous," Monk muttered.

Their next session was held in a larger room that had a few leather chairs and an enormous mahogany table at which were seated five men, two of whom—Frunzoff and Zardnov—were not strangers. Doc and his two aides pretended not to know Zardnov. The other three men at the table, it was not hard to guess, were security-police executives.

"Silence!" bellowed an SP man when Doc began a vociferous objection. "You will answer questions. That is all."

Doc Savage frowned.

The security-police officer whipped open a brief-case at his elbow, extracted a spool of recording wire—it resembled the tin spools on which adhesive tape is sold in the States—and slapped it on the table.

"This was found in your plane," the man said angrily. "It is an odd thing to be in a plane. How do you account for it?"

Doc pretended a slight surprise, said, "I shall account for nothing, naturally. This whole thing is an outrage perpetrated against an American scientist who came to Moscow to recover a strayed rocket."

"This spool was found in the plane."

"Was it?"

"It is recording wire."

"Indeed?"

The interrogator glared, shouted, and a nervous-looking Russian was pushed inside. In response to bellowed questions, he explained that in searching the plane he had found this spool of recording wire on the ship's radio-transmitter box, where it had evidently been placed for concealment.

The security-police officer swung on Doc Savage,

97

pointed at the spool, and demanded, "How does it happen there is nothing on it?"

"Isn't there?"

A Russian electronics engineer brought in a recorder, obviously an American machine, the spool was placed, and the apparatus set in operation. The result that came from the loudspeaker was not encouraging. It consisted of garbled and indecipherable quackings and whisperings.

"Merely cross-talk," Doc remarked. "The same sort of stuff is found on most recording wire when it has not been too efficiently wiped of the previous recording."

The engineer leaned over and whispered. The police official swore, turned to the man who had found the spool, and demanded, "You say this was lying on the radio-transmitter case in the plane?"

"*Da.*"

"Was the radio transmitter turned on?"

"Yes."

"Around the radio transmitter," explained the electronics expert, "there might be enough of a high-frequency field to demagnetize the wire. Since the sound is planted on the wire magnetically, the demagnetizing would naturally wipe off the wire to a greater or lesser extent, depending on how strong the field was—"

Zardnov interrupted. "Never mind the lesson in electricity. Someone in the American crew saw the ship was going to be searched, placed that spool of wire on the radio, where it would be demagnetized, and wiped out the information on the wire. Is that it?"

"That could be it."

Frunzoff looked relieved.

Zardnov waved a hand triumphantly. "At least we stopped the information they had gotten."

Frunzoff said, "There was no information. There couldn't have been. I would know it if they had questioned me, wouldn't I?"

Zardnov shrugged. "What happens to you when you are dealing with Doc Savage, who can say?" He gave the guards an order. "Take them away."

This time they were given clothes—coverall suits of coarse cloth and unlovely cut—and then taken across Communist Street, the one street inside the Kremlin, to a building beyond the tall green building called the Poteshny Dvortez, the Pleasure Palace. They were passed through a steel door, entered officially in a record book, and then urged forward again. The place was a prison. There wasn't the slightest doubt of that.

To their surprise, they were shoved into an enormous room in which there were at least a dozen other prisoners, and the door was locked behind them.

Abruptly, in Mayan, Doc said, "Pretend you do not recognize anyone here, and stick to it."

"Don't worry," Monk said. "We've been tossed in with Mahli and his bruisers." Monk spoke Mayan. He added, "Is that babe yonder the inimitable Seryi?"

"You don't know her!" Doc warned.

"Who said I did? That's the truth, too!" Monk eyed Seryi admiringly and added in English, "You know, that's a real dishy female. I wonder if she

99

would like to talk to a gentleman and a scholar?"
He sauntered toward Seryi.

The huge Mahli—he showed considerable bat-
tering at the hands of the police—came over to
Doc Savage and said bitterly, "So they got you?"

"I don't believe I understand," Doc said blankly.

"Don't give me that I-don't-know-you look,"
Mahli growled.

"Am I supposed to know you?"

Mahli considered the answer, rubbing his bruised
jaw, and finally shrugged. "I don't know who is
the fool. Me, probably." He grinned with no humor
and fell in with Doc's pretense, explaining, "You
see, three gentlemen who I had reasons for pre-
suming were Doc Savage and two associates
extracted information of value from a man named
Frunzoff. I tried to recover that information. I
failed, and in a rage, I informed the police of
the truth. They threw me and my friends in jail."

"That is interesting," Doc admitted.

Mahli, in a louder voice and for effect, added,
"I had the interests of the party at heart. The
party has made a mistake, but I am sure they
will find it out and release me. There is no man
in Russia stronger for the party than I."

Ham Brooks grinned. "Do you think that little
speech, coming in over the microphones, will
boost your stock?"

Wryly, with his lips only, Mahli said, "It doesn't
hurt to try."

"What will happen to us next?" Doc asked
curiously.

Mahli shrugged. "Usually men in this room at
noon are shot at sundown," he said.

It was cold in the room. They had been given no shoes, and the stone floor was a numbing chill against their bare feet. They sat, as some of the other prisoners were doing, cross-legged for warmth. There was not much conversation.

Monk Mayfair had managed some sort of conversation with Seryi, and seemed to get some satisfaction from the scowls Ham sent in his direction. Presently Monk rejoined them.

"She seems to be a very sweet girl," Monk said.

In English Ham said, "I'm sure she is." In Mayan, with his face as straight, he added, "I want to be around when you make your first pass at her. Five will get you twenty that they'll have to hunt for the parts."

Monk grinned. "Sour grapes."

About three o'clock, their friend from the US consulate, Clyde Warper, came to see them. He was upset and harried. "Are you all right?" he asked anxiously.

"I wouldn't call it all right," Doc said. "We are still physically intact."

"I had a hell of a time getting in to see you," Warper explained. "Things are in a mess. I'm having trouble getting word of this affair out to Washington so pressure can be put on. I've been informed the sleet storm destroyed all communication. A likely excuse."

"It's a hornet's nest," Doc agreed. "But don't get to feeling you are responsible. It was our doing, and except for an accident, we would have left Russia safely."

Clyde Warper hesitated, then said, "You've got good nerves, I hear."

101

"What do you mean?"

"I would hate to pass this information to a weak sister," Warper said, "but you can take it. Here it is: you are scheduled to be shot. The word has come straight from Stalin himself."

"That seems rather definite," Doc said.

"It's more than that. It's final." Warper moistened his lips. "There'll be plenty of hell to pay later, but I guess they're willing to risk that."

"They're not noted for being afraid to take risks."

"They're not noted for a lot of things," Clyde Warper said. "I'm going to leave you, and see how many fires I can build under swivel chairs. I don't think the fools realize the international consequences that will come from shooting you fellows."

"Do what you can," Doc said.

"I will."

When Clyde Warper had gone, Ham Brooks said, shivering, "That was an openhanded way of discussing the end of our trail. My God, I'm just beginning to realize they will shoot us. I think I knew it all along, but somehow it didn't register."

Monk shuddered and sat down. "Find a more cheerful subject, won't you!"

With a startling clanging, the steel door slammed open again, and blank-faced soldiers, rifles in hand, marched inside. Orders were shouted and the prisoners lined up.

Doc Savage found himself beside Mahli in the lineup, and the big Russian looked up at him wryly.

"The visit of your friend from the embassy was unfortunate," Mahli remarked.

"In what way?"

"In the most direct way," Mahli said. "They're going to shoot us now. Immediately."

11

Doc Savage's flake-gold eyes whipped over the faces of the prisoners, and it came to him that he was probably the only one who hadn't realized what the influx of armed soldiers meant.

Not that there was quailing before death. Most of the men had Mahli's erect cold acceptance of fate. Two or three were very pale. No face in the big stone room was wearing its natural color, probably.

Seryi stood straight, without trembling. Her face had a restraint that was complete, Madonnalike, lovely and distant. Doc looked at her wonderingly. For a fullness of steel-wrapped nerve without outward strain, he had never seen better, man or woman. Madonnalike was the description. A young woman of extreme and unusual capabilities, facing with acceptance and resignation the hell that this room would become when the rifles began smashing.

"Monk," Doc said, using the Mayan tongue, "this is going to be rough, even with all the breaks. We'll need what numbers we can get. So I'm going to team up with the other prisoners."

"All right by me."

"Get the information to Mahli. Have him pass it to the others."

"How the hell will I do that?" Monk blurted.

"I don't know. But try."

Doc Savage stepped out of the line, held up a hand, and approached the execution-squad leader. He told the man, "Get Zardnov here. Or Frunzoff. One or the other. You understand?"

The Russian had been expecting something like that, Doc surmised, although the man took his time, scowling, demanding, "For what purpose?"

"Tell them I have something to offer," Doc said. "Tell them the bargain will not be repeated. It is now or never."

The Russian laughed. "Now or never—I would say so too." However, he swung, snapped a command at a junior to take over, and left the execution room, the door being carefully unlocked, then locked behind him again.

Zardnov had been waiting nearby, obviously. He appeared in brisk order, but said coldly, "I happened to be passing. They were lucky to catch me. What is this nonsense?"

"There was a spool containing wire," Doc said.

"You admit that, then?"

Doc shrugged. "I wish to make a deal."

"What deal?"

"The obvious one—for my life and those of my friends."

"And so?"

"Don't be coy with me, Zardnov," Doc said coldly. "This is of quite an importance to you. Stalin is involved, and a great deal of ill feeling throughout the Council. I imagine the gossip is already around, and it isn't going to do the regime any good." Doc eyed the man intently, and added,

"You, I imagine, are not uninterested in the existence of Frunzoff as a prepared successor to—"

"Shut up!" Zardnov blurted. He came close to Doc Savage, adding, "Lower your voice, you fool. If you knew the bitter feeling among the Central Committee members—"

Doc reached out, seized the man, jerked him close, and slapped a hand against the anesthetic-gas grenade which he had planted in the show handkerchief in Zardnov's breast coat pocket during the mysterious goings-on at the airport when the smoke grenade had been "accidentally" detonated by Doc's double.

Doc held his breath.

He turned his head, saw Mahli wheel wildly and whisper to the man next to him in the line of prisoners. An order, Doc knew, to hold his breath for as long as possible, and to pass the instruction down the line.

The trained reaction was wonderful to watch. Doc recalled how Seryi, earlier in the night, had said that Mahli was a top agent and that his men were superior. She had not exaggerated. No questions were asked. Obedience was instant and complete. The word to hold breaths went down the line faster than a gossip rumor.

It held, even when a guard shot two prisoners in cold blood with his rifle. That happened after the guards and execution squad began to fold down on the floor.

Zardnov was already loose in Doc's arms. Doc frisked him hurriedly, taking what documents he

107

could find, and particularly Zardnov's diplomatic papers and local police passes. They might be handy.

Counting seconds mentally until they reached a minute, Doc released his breath, said in Russian, "Let's go. Get into Communist Street, turn left, and there will be two cars parked near the Poteshny Dvortez. The keys will be in them. Leave no one behind. The cars are armored. Make for the Tanitzkiye Gate."

Mahli blurted, "This was arranged?"

"Come on," Doc said curtly. "This was planned for months. There are escapes prepared from every predicament we could visualize."

Mahli grinned an ugly grin. "You are not disappointing me after all, Mr. Savage." He wheeled and bellowed at his men to be sure to grab ammunition for the rifles they were taking off the gassed guards.

Going down a hall, Seryi ranged alongside Doc Savage and asked wonderingly, "How did you plant the gas grenade on Zardnov? It was a gas grenade, was it not?"

"Yes. It was put there earlier. At the airport."

"But you asked the executioner for Frunzoff. Suppose he had come instead of Zardnov?"

"There was a plant in every suit of clothes Frunzoff had," Doc said. "We arranged that last night while we were working on him."

"I'm beginning to think you are infallible."

"Only every other hour," Doc said. "Or I wouldn't be here. We're not out of it, you know."

In the ancient thoroughfare that was the only street in the Kremlin, they ran in a compact group.

Doc noted that Mahli snapped an order, and his men moved to positions which ringed Doc, Monk, Ham, and Seryi. Mahli said wryly, "We're not ungrateful. This is a protective measure, not a device to surround you."

"Never mind the gratitude," Doc said rapidly. "Before we get out of this—yonder are the cars. I hope they hold everybody."

"They will, under the circumstances," Mahli said.

The shooting began now. Sporadic at first, three or four spaced reports, then a flurry or two. Then it stopped.

They jammed into the cars. Doc, Monk, Ham, Seryi, and some others took one machine. Mahli and the rest wedged into the other touring car. Mahli shouted, "After we are past the gate, let me lead. You may know Moscow, but not the way I know it, I assure you."

The shooting started anew. Two bullets came into their car, smashing windows, and a man threw his body back in an arching bend and made ghastly mewing sounds.

"Keep down," Doc said. "The car bodies are armor steel. Or were supposed to be."

He slid down himself. He was driving. The plan —originally it had envisaged nothing as elaborate as this break—was for them to leave through the Tanitzkiye Gate, where only one guard was stationed. There was even an arrangement for an American secret agent who had operated a fruit concession nearby for several weeks to shoot down the guard if necessary. It didn't prove needed. One of Mahli's men shot him expertly long before they reached the gate.

The cars piled ahead wildly, reeling through the small landscaped park, swinging in sharp turns. Mahli led, and he, as he had said, knew the streets. He chose with an uncanny facility those which were least slotted with traffic, not a mean accomplishment at this hour of the day.

In the western business area, Mahli's car swerved to the right and dived into an arched areaway. Men were leaning out, beckoning Doc's party to follow. They did so.

Unloading from the cars in haste, they sprinted through doors and hallways, Mahli finally turning through a door which proved to be the rear entrance to a tailor shop presided over by a very fat and very startled tailor. The proprietor barked anxiously at Mahli.

Mahli told Doc, "There are security-police uniforms here to fit everyone. In a tailor shop? Why not?" He slapped the fat tailor on the back. "Ivan is a resourceful fellow."

Doc said, "You keep a few aces in your sleeve too, I see."

Mahli nodded. "In Russia today, who can tell when it will be very convenient to look like a soldier? You will find credentials in each, incidentally."

The tailor seized Doc's arm excitedly. He was not, he yelled, certain that he had a uniform large enough for Doc. A uniform for a large man, yes. But a large man with a great belly, if he did possibly have one.

He had one uniform long enough, and as the tailor said, it had an excess of midriff.

Mahli came over to Doc.

"There is another car near here which you can

use," he said. "It is an army vehicle. It will fit well with the uniforms."

"Fine."

"I would like to suggest," Mahli added, "in view of the hell all of Russia is going to be for you in an hour or two, that you try the bold way."

"The airport?"

Mahli nodded. "The crew of your plane are being held there." Mahli described the spot, explaining the information had come from his tailor friend. "I'm confident, having seen you function, that you can free them, get to your plane, and take off."

"Thanks."

"It is a favor," Mahli said. "You could return it, you know."

"How?"

"I am an ambitious man," Mahli said. "The present regime will not last forever, and after that, who can say? Maybe an ambitious young fellow like myself, no? . . . It would be a help to me if I knew whether Frunzoff is the man prepared for the number-one spot."

"He is," Doc said.

"Thank you." Mahli was deeply grateful. "The information makes Frunzoff a very poor insurance risk, I can assure you."

Doc frowned. "That sort of violence is never going to establish security for Russia."

There was a thin fierceness behind Mahli's grin. "We shall see. Perhaps I could become a tame man."

"It would be worth considering."

Seryi stood beside Doc Savage. "Mahli is quite

ā man," she said softly. "He has qualities you have not observed."

Doc looked at her, his admiration suddenly frank. "So have you, if I may say so. A new one, a little more titanic than the predecessors, develops each time I meet you, it seems."

Mahli laughed. "I imagine my lovely cousin has ā wish that this thing of meetings and developments continues."

Seryi reddened and said bitingly, "Tact is something you could acquire, you big lout."

Mahli roared. "What is the thing that loses a man a woman quickest? Why, tact!"

The tailor came bustling up. "The army car is ready," he said. "I would not advise a full day of gossip."

12

Doc Savage left his headquarters on the eighty-sixth floor of a midtown New York skyscraper, rode a taxi to the rather snobbish club on upper Fifth Avenue where Ham Brooks lived, and found Ham arguing the merits of a recent Supreme Court case with another attorney.

"We'll pick up Monk." Doc consulted his watch. "We've not too much time. The conference at Lake Success is at three o'clock."

"Monk will be at the Corona Theater on Forty-seventh Street," Ham said.

"I'll drive by."

"Monk," said Ham, grinning, "has staged the damnedest recovery in the ten days since we got out of Moscow. He's convinced some guy he is considering angeling a show, and that lets him hang around rehearsals. Imagine that! Monk couldn't bankroll a decent suit of clothes right now. But you can guess his angle. It's a musical they're rehearsing. Babes."

"Maybe he'd rather miss this."

Ham shook his head quickly. "No. Not this. Monk has great feeling for our old pal Zardnov."

Monk, when they found him, expressed the same sentiment. "I hear our old pal Zardnov hit town last night," he said. "When are we going out to see old pal Zardnov?"

"Right now," Doc explained. "There has been a United Nations committee all set up and waiting."

The room at Lake Success was small, pleasant except for a reek of cigar smoke that was just a trifle too thin to saw up in blocks.

Zardnov jumped to his feet, glaring, when Doc Savage arrived. The committee had been giving Zardnov a hard time of it, evidently. Zardnov whacked a desk with his cane.

"I demand," Zardnov shouted at Doc, "that you here and now admit as lies all that you have told this committee pertaining—"

"Sit down," Doc said curtly. "You're talking about the incident ten days ago in Moscow, presumably?"

"There was no incident!" Zardnov bellowed.

Monk asked, "What do you guys call an incident over there?"

Doc addressed Zardnov. "I presume you expect me to make a denial that there exists a man named Frunzoff who has been prepared for heading the Russian government in an emergency, and accordingly has more complete knowledge of Russian affairs, particularly the atom-bomb situation, than any other man in Russia other than you-know-who?"

"A lie," said Zardnov. "I categorically and specifically deny—"

"Let's shorten this," Doc said. "We have a wire recording of an interview with Frunzoff, given under the influence of some very fine truth serum. The information in the recording, I can assure you, is going to be very disastrous to Russia."

"That also is untrue—"

"Remember at the airport in Moscow when the smoke grenade went off by accident?" Doc asked.

"Accident!" Zardnov exploded. "The purpose of that was to conceal your silly gas bomb in my clothing!"

Doc shook his head. "It had two purposes. . . . Get his cane, Monk."

Monk walked over, Zardnov raised the cane to strike at the homely chemist, and Monk made a quick feint and got it. Zardnov swore. Monk laughed and retreated with the cane.

"Such hoodlum acts," Zardnov screamed, "are below the dignity of an international body of this type. I demand the arrest of these men."

Monk was inspecting the cane. He gripped it in his powerful hands, twisted, and began to unscrew the top section.

Zardnov's eyes protruded. "That cane is supposed to be solid ironwood—"

"It's not your original cane, Zardnov," Doc told him wearily. "This one, an exact imitation, and I do mean exact, was made several weeks ago when you were in the hospital with a bad cold, and the cane was accessible to us for periods of time."

Zardnov looked sick. Wordless.

"The recorder wire is inside the cane," Doc assured him. "You brought it from Moscow yourself."

Zardnov sat down very slowly and carefully, seeming not to notice that there was no chair.

AFTERWORD
by Will Murray

Doc Savage fans have already realized that *The Red Spider* is unusual. This grim, suspenseful tale of Cold War espionage is a quantum jump ahead of anything Lester Dent wrote under the name Kenneth Robeson. *The Red Spider* is the one Doc Savage adventure which Lester Dent thought would never see print. Dent undoubtedly considered it one of the finest Doc stories he ever wrote, and so did his editors. Although this novel *was* purchased for *Doc Savage* magazine in 1948, it never appeared there. This was the only Doc Savage story killed by editorial decision—not because it was an unacceptable story but because it was *too* good a story.

One has the sense, upon reading *The Red Spider*, that many years have passed in the careers of Doc Savage and his men. This is an older, more brittle, Doc Savage—not the noble bronze superman of the depression era. He still possesses the same bronze coloring, flake-gold eyes, great strength and gadgets, but he has changed. He has broken himself of his habit of trilling, and he is now an international troubleshooter for the American government. Even his men have changed. They are attached to the military.

The familiar characters are recognizable, but they

exist in a world that is technologically and political-
ly closer to our own. This is a world of rockets,
radar, atomic weapons and the Iron Curtain. Gone
are the fantastic adventures, stratosphere dirigibles
and evil supercriminals. In their place is realism,
and Doc and his men are necessarily depicted in
more realistic terms themselves.

The Doc Savage milleau has matured.

Dent's familiar offbeat humor has given way to
suspense, and his characters are now allowed rare
emotional dimension. This maturing had been going on in the pages of *Doc Savage* since 1943, but
Lester Dent never quite achieved the perfect balance between realism and larger-than-life characterization until *The Red Spider*. This is the ultimate
Doc Savage adventure.

Lester Dent alone is not responsible for the combined elements which make this such an exemplary
story. Actually, this novel is a fusion of Dent's ideas
and those of the various editors whose attitudes
changed and shaped the adventures over the years.

There was only one editor during the first decade
of *Doc Savage*. He was John L. Nanovic, and he
planned every adventure with Lester Dent and ap-
proved all of Dent's story outlines. Nanovic was
also responsible for maintaining the consistency of
Doc's superhuman characterization. This is the Doc
Savage—the invincible Man of Bronze—who is familiar to most readers.

In 1943, Charles Moran, the first of several short-
term editors, replaced Nanovic. Moran did not like
Dent's fantastic plots or his portrayal of Doc Savage
as a superman. Moran instructed Dent to play down
those elements, including Doc's gadgets, and to play
up suspense and realism instead. These changes

became the foundation for all subsequent Doc stories. Moran's editorial legacy is evident in *The Red Spider*.

William de Grouchy, who replaced Moran, did not alter this policy greatly. During de Grouchy's term, however, Lester Dent developed a new type of Doc story line, perhaps at de Grouchy's suggestion. These stories involved Doc in World War II espionage assignments in which he and his men infiltrated enemy territory. These missions were highly suspenseful because their completion was only half the story. The other half, often the more difficult, was to get back to Allied territory without being captured and shot as spies. When the war ended, so did this story line, but Dent revived it in *The Red Spider*.

For Lester Dent, who claimed that he wrote Doc Savage best, "when I gallop through it as if on a picnic, a mood which often makes it hard to get fearsome, but makes swell entertainment," this emphasis on suspense was a difficult transition to make. Many of these war-time stories "came hard," he claimed, but his extra effort resulted in some excellent adventures.

The next *Doc Savage* editor was a woman named Babette Rosmond. Her interests were in detective fiction and sophisticated writing. She retitled the magazine *Doc Savage, Science Detective*, and Dent accordingly recast the Man of Bronze as a sort of private investigator of the unusual. Dent's style changed dramatically in the novels he wrote for Rosmond. The stories show polish, humor, mature characterization and a willingness to experiment. *The Red Spider* is written in this style.

Though Doc and his aides became free-lance investigators, they continued to undertake missions for the government. Twice in 1947, they became embroiled in political intrigue. They quelled a Middle Eastern holy war in *Danger Lies East* and headed off World War III in *Terror Wears No Shoes*. The latter story hinted that Russia was behind the trouble. Doc Savage was slowly emerging as the archenemy of world Communism.

Doc Savage, Science Detective was not selling well in early 1948, and William de Grouchy was brought back to salvage the dying magazine. De Grouchy decided that it was time for a return to the original larger-than-life Doc Savage, gadgets and all. He asked Lester Dent for a story that did this without sacrificing realism or good writing.

In April, 1948, Lester Dent wrote a story he called "In Hell, Madonna." The plot used the historical backdrop of that brief period when America was the sole atomic power. As Dent described in a now-ironic note attached to his outline for the story:

This one is laid against a background of international trouble that should be even more in the public eye about the time it is published —the question of whether or not the Soviet has the atom bomb.

It isn't a bomb story, because the bomb doesn't appear. And for the sake of the few specks of international courtesy still floating around, I suppose it would do no harm not to name Soviet Russia definitely as the locale.

Anyway, Doc and his aides have simply been assigned the job of finding the answer to the question that is on a few minds over here. Have they got the bomb over there?

This story is, of course, *The Red Spider*. Evidently de Grouchy thought that there was no point in beating around the bush where the Russian locale was concerned. He seems to have liked everything about "In Hell, Madonna" except the title, which is a phrase out of Shakespeare's *Twelfth Night*. De Grouchy asked Dent for a better title and Dent offered six alternates, "Kill in Moscow," "Mr. Calamity," "One Man Screaming," "Moscow Maneuver," "The Red Night," and "The Prince in Red."

Which of these titles de Grouchy would have used remains an unanswered question because, before he could schedule the story for *Doc Savage, Science Detective*, he was replaced by a new editor, Daisy Bacon.

Daisy Bacon killed the story. She was an old-line pulp editor who, like de Grouchy, wanted to see *Doc Savage* return to its former glory. But she wanted nothing of sophisticated writing or, as she instructed Lester Dent, Cold War tales:

> The firm wishes to give the European situation a miss and I would rule it out myself anyway because the public is thoroughly fed up with politics and propaganda in fiction. I don't know where the idea of Doc Savage saving the world came from but I suppose it is a hangover from the One World idea.

And that was that. Daisy Bacon put the story on the shelf. As *Doc Savage* was just shifting from a bi-monthly to a quarterly publication, she simply *skipped* the issue for which it was intended, and Doc readers never suspected a thing!

Whether Daisy Bacon ever intended to publish

The Red Spider is unknown. Probably not, because, its political theme aside, the novel was simply *too* sophisticated for her vision of *Doc Savage*. The question is a moot one, as the magazine only lasted another three issues, effectively ending any hope Lester Dent had for its publication. With his death in 1959, the very existence of the manuscript was forgotten.

Forgotten, that is, until 1975, when I went looking through the Street & Smith files (now held by Condé Nast) in the course of researching an article on the Doc Savage authors titled, "The Secret Kenneth Robesons." In those dusty files, I found records of what appeared to be a hitherto unknown Doc Savage novel. With the kind permission of Condé Nast's Paul H. Bonner, I undertook a search for the manuscript.

It took two years until the only surviving copy —a carbon—was located among Lester Dent's papers. Finally, in 1978, I closed an agreement between Condé Nast, Bantam Books and Mrs. Norma Dent, permitting the manuscript to be published.

And here it is, under a new title, *The Red Spider* —the ultimate Doc Savage adventure. It stands as the high-water mark in the series, in which Doc Savage is realized as a *realistic* superman in one of his most dramatic exploits.

Because this is one of the last Doc Savage adventures, *The Red Spider* is remarkable in a number of other ways. This is the Man of Bronze's only adventure set in Russia. It is also his first open confrontation with the Communist threat, and it indicates a direction in which Lester Dent intended to take Doc's crusade against injustice, had it not been for the editorial injunction against Cold War stories.

In the beautiful and eerie second chapter, Doc makes his first recorded supersonic flight.

Except for Monk and Ham, most of Doc's aides rarely appeared in the final years. This adventure is Renny Renwick's and Long Tom Roberts' final exploit with the bronze man.

As for the madonna of Dent's original title, the intriguing Seryi Mitroff, she is a rare example of the kind of capable woman who actually attracts the otherwise womanproof Doc Savage. It is an interesting and little-known insight into Doc's personality that the only other women who interested him, Princess Monja in *The Man of Bronze* and Rhoda Haven in *The Freckled Shark*, are both described as the madonna-like type. One can only wonder if Lester Dent ever planned another encounter between Seryi Mitroff and Doc Savage.

It is unfortunate that no more Doc stories of the caliber and distinction of *The Red Spider* were written. Nevertheless, Doc Savage fans everywhere can be thankful that this lost adventure has been rescued from obscurity, for it is one of Lester Dent's finest. It is fitting, too, that the first new Doc Savage story to be published—exactly thirty years to the month since the last one—should appear under the imprint of Bantam Books, who have resurrected the Man of Bronze for a new generation of readers.

A SPECIAL PREVIEW OF
THE SHATTERING OPENING PAGES
OF A NEW NOVEL OF RELENTLESS
TERROR

THE WOLFEN
by
Whitley Strieber

WARNING:

Here are the first pages from a new novel
that will frighten many readers. Do not
turn the page unless you are prepared for
a graphic description of the elemental ter-
rors that lurk unseen in the darkness of
city streets.

In Brooklyn they take abandoned cars to the Fountain Avenue Automobile Pound adjacent to the Fountain Avenue Dump. The pound and the dump occupy land shown on maps as "Spring Creek Park (Proposed)." There is no spring, no creek, and no park.

Normally the pound is silent, its peace disturbed only by an occasional fight among the packs of wild dogs that roam there, or perhaps the cries of the sea gulls that hover over the stinking, smoldering dump nearby.

The members of the Police Auto Squad who visit the pound to mark derelicts for the crusher do not consider the place dangerous. Once in a while the foot-long rats will get aggressive and become the victims of target practice. The scruffy little wild dogs will also attack every so often, but they can usually be dealt with by a shot into the ground. Auto-pound duty consists of marking big white X's on the worst of the derelicts and taking Polaroids of them to prove that they were beyond salvage in case any owners turn up.

It isn't the kind of job that the men associate with danger, much less getting killed, so Hugo DiFalco and Dennis Houlihan would have laughed in your face if you told them they had only three minutes to live when they heard the first sound behind them.

"What was that?" Houlihan asked. He was bored and wouldn't have minded getting a couple of shots off at a rat.

"A noise."

"Brilliant. That's what I thought it was too."

They both laughed. Then there was another sound, a staccato growl that ended on a murmuring high note. The two men looked at one another. "That sounds like my brother singing in the shower," DiFalco said.

From ahead of them came further sounds—rustlings and more of the unusual growls. Di-

Falco and Houlihan stopped. They weren't joking anymore, but they also weren't afraid, only curious. The wet, ruined cars just didn't seem to hold any danger on this dripping autumn afternoon. But there was something out there.

They were now in the center of a circle of half-heard rustling movement. As both men realized that something had surrounded them, they had their first twinge of concern. They now had less than one minute of life remaining. Both of them lived with the central truth of police work —it could happen anytime. But what the hell was happening now?

Then something stepped gingerly from between two derelicts and stood facing the victims.

The men were not frightened, but they sensed danger. As it had before in moments of peril, Hugo DiFalco's mind turned to a brief thought of his wife, of how she liked to say "We're an us." Dennis Houlihan felt a shiver of prickles come over him as if the hair all over his body was standing up.

"Don't move, man," DiFalco said.

It snarled at the voice. "There's more of 'em behind us, buddy." Their voices were low and controlled, the tone of professionals in trouble. They moved closer together; their shoulders touched. Both men knew that one of them had to turn around, the other keep facing this way. But they didn't need to talk about it; they had worked together too long to have to plan their moves.

DiFalco started to make the turn and draw his pistol. That was the mistake.

Ten seconds later their throats were being torn out. Twenty seconds later the last life was pulsing out of their bodies. Thirty seconds later they were being systematically consumed.

Neither man had made a sound, Houlihan

had seen the one in front of them twitch its eyes, but before he could follow the movement there was a searing pain in his throat and he was suddenly, desperately struggling for air through the bubbling torrent of his own blood.

DiFalco's hand had just gripped the familiar checkered wooden butt of his service revolver when it was yanked violently aside. The impression of impossibly fast-moving shapes entered his astonished mind, then something slammed into his chest and he too was bleeding, in his imagination protecting his throat as in reality his body slumped to the ground and his mind sank into darkness.

The attackers moved almost too quickly, their speed born of nervousness at the youth of their victims. The shirts were torn open, the white chests exposed, the entrails tugged out and taken away, the precious organs swallowed. The rest was left behind.

In less than five more minutes it was over. The hollow, ravaged corpses lay there in the mud, two ended lives now food for the wild scavengers of the area.

For a long time nothing more moved at the Fountain Avenue Automobile Pound. The cries of gulls echoed among the rustling hulks of the cars. Around the corpses the blood coagulated and blackened. As the afternoon drew on, the autumn mist became rain, covering the dead policemen with droplets of water and making the blood run again.

Night fell.

Rats worried the corpses until dawn.

The two men had been listed AWOL for fourteen hours. Most unusual for these guys. They were both family types, steady and reliable. AWOL wasn't their style. But still, what could happen to two experienced policemen on marking duty at the auto pound? That was a question nobody would even try to answer until a search was made for the men.

Police work might be dangerous, but nobody seriously believed that DiFalco and Houlihan were in any real trouble. Maybe there had been a family emergency and the two had failed to check in. Maybe a lot of things. And maybe there *was* some trouble. Nobody realized that the world had just become a much more dangerous place, and they wouldn't understand that for quite some time. Right now they were just looking for a couple of missing policemen. Right now the mystery began and ended with four cops poking through the auto pound for signs of their buddies.

"They better not be sleeping in some damn car." Secretly all four men hoped that the two AWOL officers were off on a bender or something. You'd rather see that than the other possibility.

A cop screamed. The sound stunned the other three to silence because it was one they rarely heard.

"Over here," the rookie called in a choking voice.

"Hold on, man." The other three converged on the spot as the rookie's cries sounded again and again. When the older men got there he slumped against a car.

The three older cops cursed.

"Call the hell in. Get Homicide out here. Seal the area. Jesus Christ!"

They covered the remains with their rainslickers. They put their hats where the faces had been.

The police communications network responded fast; fellow officers were dead, nobody wasted time. Ten minutes after the initial alarms had gone out the phone was ringing in the half-empty ready-room of the Brooklyn Homicide Division. Detective Becky Neff picked it up. "Neff," the gruff voice of the Inspector said, "you and Wilson're assigned to a case in the Seventy-fifth Precinct."

"The what?"

"It's the Fountain Avenue Dump. Got a double cop killing, mutilation, probable sex assault, cannibalism. Get the hell out there fast." The line clicked.

"Wake up, George, we've got a case," Neff growled. "We've got a bad one." She had hardly absorbed what the Inspector had said—mutilation and cannibalism? What in the name of God had happened out there? "Somebody killed two cops and cannibalized them."

Wilson, who had been resting in a tilted-back chair after a grueling four-hour paperwork session, leaned forward and got to his feet.

"Let's go. Where's the scene?"

"Fountain Avenue Dump. Seventy-fifth Precinct."

"Goddamn out-of-the-way place." He shook his head. "Guys must have gotten themselves jumped."

They went down to Becky Neff's old blue Pontiac and set the flasher up on the dashboard. She pulled the car out of its parking place and edged into the dense traffic of downtown Brooklyn. Wilson flipped on the radio and reported to the dispatcher. "Siren's working," Wilson commented as he flipped the toggle switch. The siren responded with an electronic warble, and he grunted with satisfaction; it had been on the blink for over a month, and there had been no response from the repair unit. Budget cuts had reduced this once-efficient team to exactly twelve men for the entire fleet of police vehicles. Unmarked cars were low on the list of precedence for flasher and siren repairs.

"I fixed it," Becky Neff said, "and I'm damn glad now." The ride to the car pound would be made much easier by the siren, and time could not be wasted.

Wilson raised his eyebrows. "You fixed it?"

"I borrowed the manual and fixed it. Nothing to it." Actually she had gotten a neighborhood electronics freak to do the job, a guy with a computer in his living room. But there was no reason to let Wilson know that.

"You fixed it," Wilson said again.

"You're repeating yourself."

He shook his head.

As the car swung onto the Brooklyn-Queens Expressway he used the siren, flipping the toggle to generate a series of startling whoops that cleared something of a path for them. But traffic was even worse as they approached the Battery Tunnel interchange, and the siren did little good in the confusion of trucks and buses. "Step on it, Becky."

"I'm stepping. You're working the siren."

"I don't care what you do, but move!"

His outburst made her want to snap back at him, but she understood how he felt. She shared his emotions and knew his anger was directed at the road. Cop killings made you hate the world, and the damn city in particular.

Wilson leaned out of his window and shouted at the driver of a truck stuck in the middle of the lane. "Police! Get that damn thing moving or you're under arrest!"

The driver shot the finger but moved the vehicle. Becky Neff jammed her accelerator to the floor, skidding around more slowly moving traffic, at times breaking into the clear, at times stuck again.

As the dashboard clock moved through the better part of an hour they approached their destination. They got off the B-Q-E and went straight out Flatbush Avenue, into the sometimes seedy, sometimes neat residential areas beyond. The precincts rolled by, the 78th, the 77th, the 73rd. Finally they entered the 75th and turned onto Flatlands Avenue, a street of nondescript shops in a racially mixed lower-and middle-income neighborhood. The 75th was as average a precinct as there was in New York. About a hundred thousand people lived there, not many poor and not many rich, and about evenly divided between black, white, and Hispanic.

The 75th was the kind of precinct you never read about in the papers, the kind of place where policemen lived out good solid careers without ever shooting a man—not the kind of place where they got killed, much elss mutilated and cannibalized.

Finally they turned onto Fountain Avenue. In the distance a little clutch of flashers could be seen in the dismal autumn light—that must mark the official vehicles pulled up to the entrance of the Automobile Pound. The scene of the crime. And judging from the news cars careening down the street, the 75th Precinct wasn't going to be an obscure place much longer.

"Who's Precinct Captain?" Neff asked her superior officer. Wilson was senior man on the team, a fact which he was careful to make sure she never forgot. He also had a terrific memory for details.

"Gerardi, I think, something Gerardi. Good enough cop. The place is tight s'far as I know.

Nothin' much going on. It's not Midtown South, if you know what I mean."

"Yeah." What Wilson meant was that this precinct was clean—no bad cops, no mob connections, no serious graft. Unlike Midtown South there wasn't even the opportunity.

"Sounds like it's a psycho case to me," Neff said. She was always careful to pick her words when she theorized around Wilson. He was scathing when he heard poorly thought out ideas and had no tolerance for people with less skill than he himself possessed. Which was to say, he was intolerant of almost the entire police force. He was probably the best detective in Homocide, maybe the best on the force. He was also lazy, venal, inclined toward a Victorian view of women, and a profound slob. Except for their abilities in the craft of police detection, Becky liked to think they had nothing in common. Where Wilson was a slob, Becky tended to be orderly. She was always the one who kept at the paperwork when Wilson gave up, and who kept the dreary minutiae of their professional lives organized.

She and Wilson didn't exactly dislike one another—it was more than that, it was pure hate laced with grudging respect. Neff thought that Wilson was a Stone Age chauvinist and was revolted by the clerical role he often forced her to play—and he considered her a female upstart in a profession where women were at best a mistake.

But they were both exceptional detectives, and that kept them together. Neff couldn't help but admire her partner's work, and he had been forced to admit that she was one of the few officers he had encountered who could keep up with him.

The fact that Becky Neff was also not a bad-looking thirty-four had helped as well. Wilson was a bachelor, over fifty and not much more appealing physically than a busted refrigerator (which he resembled in shape and height). Becky saw from the first that she was attractive to him, and she played it up a little, believing that her progress in her career was more important than whether or not she let Wilson flirt with her. But it went no further than that. Becky's husband Dick was also on the force, a captain in Narcotics, and Wilson wouldn't mess around with another cop's wife.

The idea of Wilson messing around with anybody was ridiculous anyway; he had remained a bachelor partly out of choice and partly because few women would tolerate his arrogance and his sloppy indifference to even the most fundamental social graces, like taking the meat out of a hamburger and eating it separately, which was one of his nicer table manners.

"Let's just go blank on this one, sweetheart," Wilson rumbled. "We don't know what the hell happened out there."

"Cannibalism would indicate—"

"We don't know. Guys are excited, maybe it was something else. Let's just find what we find."

Becky pulled the car in among the official vehicles and snapped her folding umbrella out of her purse. She opened it against the rain and was annoyed to see Wilson go trudging off into the mud, pointedly ignoring his own comfort. "Let the bastard catch pneumonia," she thought as she huddled forward beneath the umbrella. Wilson was a great one for appearances—he gets to the scene wet, indifferent to his own comfort, concerned only with the problem at hand, while his dainty little partner follows along behind with her umbrella, carefully mincing over the puddles. Ignoring him as best she could, she set off toward the kliegs that now lit the scene of the murders some fifty yards into the area.

As soon as she saw the mess she knew that this was no normal case. Something that made you break out in a sweat even in this weather had happened to these men. She glanced at Wilson, surprised to see that even old superpro's eyes were opened wide with surprise. "Jesus," he said, "I mean . . . what?"

The Precinct Captain came forward. "We don't know, sir," he said to Wilson, acknowledging the other man's seniority and fame on the force. And he also eyed Becky Neff, well-known enough in her own right as one of the most visible female officers in New York. Her picture had appeared in the *Daily News* more than once in connection with some of her and Wilson's more spectacular cases. Wilson shunned the photographers himself—or they shunned him, it was hard to say which. But Becky welcomed them, highly conscious of her role as living and visible proof that female officers could work the front lines as well as their male counterparts.

Taking a deep breath she knelt down beside the corpses while Wilson was still registering his shock. Every fiber of her body wanted to run, to get away from the unspeakable horror before her—but instead she looked closely, peering at the broken, gristle-covered bones and the dark lumps of flesh that seemed almost to glow beneath the lights that had been set up by the Forensics officers.

"Where the hell's the Medical Examiner?"

Wilson said behind her. A voice answered. Wilson did not come any closer; she knew that he wasn't going to because he couldn't stomach this sort of thing. Clenching her teeth against her own disgust, she stared at the bodies, noting the most unusual thing about them—the long scrape marks on the exposed bones and the general evidence of gnawing. She stood up and looked around the desolate spot. About a quarter of a mile away the dump could be seen with huge flocks of sea gulls hovering over the mounds of garbage. Even over the hubbub of voices you could hear the gulls screaming. From here to the dump was an ocean of old cars and trucks of every imaginable description, most of them worthless, stripped hulks. A few nearby had white X's on the windshields or hoods, evidence of the work DiFalco and Houlihan had been doing when the attack occurred.

"They were gnawed by rats," Becky said in as level a tone as she could manage, "but those larger marks indicate something else—dogs?"

"The wild dogs around here are just scrawny little mutts," the Precinct Captain said.

"How long were these men missing before you instituted a search, Captain?" Wilson asked.

The Captain glanced sharply at him. Neff was amazed; nobody below the rank of Inspector had the right to ask a captain a question like that, and even then not outside of a Board of Inquiry. It was a question that belonged in a dereliction of duty hearing, not at the scene of a crime.

"We need to know," Wilson added a little too loudly.

"Then ask the M. E. how long they've been dead. We found them two hours ago. Figure the rest out for yourself." The Captain turned away, and Becky Neff followed his gaze out over the distant Atlantic, where a helicopter could be seen growing rapidly larger. It was a police chopper and it was soon above them, its rotor clattering as it swung around looking for a likely spot to land.

"That's the Commissioner and the Chief," Wilson said. "They must have smelled newsmen." In January a new mayor would take office, and senior city officials were all scrambling to keep their jobs. So these normally anonymous men now jumped at the possibility of getting their faces on the eleven o'clock news. But this time they would be disappointed—because of the unusually hideous nature of the crime, the press was being kept as far away as possible. No pictures allowed until the scene was cleared of the bodies.

At the same time that the Chief of Detectives and the Commissioner were getting out of their helicopter, the Medical Examiner was hurrying across the muddy ground with a newspaper folded up and held over his head against the rain. "It's Evans himself," Wilson said. "I haven't seen that man outdoors in twenty years."

"I'm glad he's here."

Evans was the city's Chief Medical Examiner, a man renowned for his ingenious feats of forensic detection. He rolled along, shabby, tiny, looking very old behind his thick glasses.

He had worked with Wilson and Neff often and greeted them both with a nod. "What's your idea?" he said even before examining the bodies. Most policemen he treated politely enough; these two he respected.

"We're going to have a problem finding the cause of death," Wilson said, "because of the shape they're in."

Evans nodded. "Is Forensics finished with the bodies?" The Forensics team was finished, which meant that the corpses could be touched. Dr. Evans rolled on his black rubber gloves and bent down. So absorbed did he become that he didn't even acknowledge the approach of the brass.

The group watched Evans as he probed gingerly at the bodies. Later he would do a much more thorough autopsy in his lab, but these first impressions were important and would be his only on-site inspection of the victims.

When he backed away from the bodies, his face was registering confusion. "I don't understand this at all," he said slowly. "These men have been killed by . . . something with claws, teeth. Animals of some kind. But what doesn't make sense is—why didn't they defend themselves?"

"Their guns aren't even drawn," Becky said through dry lips. It was the first thing she had noticed.

"Maybe that wasn't the mode of death, Doctor," Wilson said. "I mean, maybe they were killed first and then eaten by the animals around here. There's rats, gulls, also some wild dogs, the precinct boys say."

The doctor pursed his lips. He nodded. "We'll find out when we do the autopsy. Maybe you're right, but on the surface I'd say we're looking at the fatal wounds."

The Forensics team was photographing and marking the site, picking up scattered remains and vacuuming the area as well as possible considering the mud. They also took impressions of the multitude of pawprints that surrounded the bodies.

The Precinct Captain finally broke the silence. "You're saying that these guys were killed by wild dogs, and they didn't even draw their guns? That can't be right. Those dogs are just little things—they're not even a nuisance." He looked around. "Anybody ever hear of a death from wild dogs in the city? Anybody?"

These brutal murders are just the first of many violent deaths that puzzle the New York Police. Who are these mysterious killers who stalk helpless human prey? IF YOU ARE AFRAID TO FINISH THIS STORY, YOU ARE NOT ALONE.

(The complete Bantam Book is on sale June 20th, wherever paperbacks are sold.)

To the world at large, Doc Savage is a strange, mysterious figure of glistening bronze skin and golden eyes. To his fans he is the greatest adventure hero of all time, whose fantastic exploits are unequaled for hair-raising thrills, breathtaking escapes, blood-curdling excitement!

☐ 11317	MURDER MELODY	$1.25
☐ 11318	SPOOK LEGION	$1.25
☐ 11320	THE SARGASSO OGRE	$1.25
☐ 11321	THE PIRATE OF THE PACIFIC	$1.25
☐ 11322	THE SECRET IN THE SKY	$1.25
☐ 11248	THE AWFUL EGG	$1.50
☐ 11191	TUNNEL TERROR	$1.50
☐ 12780	THE HATE GENIUS	$1.75
☐ 11116	THE PURPLE DRAGON	$1.25
☐ 12787	THE RED SPIDER	$1.75

FANTASY AND SCIENCE FICTION FAVORITES

Bantam brings you the recognized classics as well as the current favorites in fantasy and science fantasy. Here you will find the beloved Conan books along with recent titles by the most respected authors in the genre.

☐	10031	NOVA Samuel R. Delany	$1.75
☐	12680	TRITON Samuel R. Delany	$2.25
☐	11718	DHALGREN Samuel R. Delany	$2.25
☐	11950	ROGUE IN SPACE Frederic Brown	$1.75
☐	12018	CONAN THE SWORDSMAN #1	
		DeCamp & Carter	$1.95
☐	12706	CONAN THE LIBERATOR #2	
		DeCamp & Carter	$1.95
☐	12031	SKULLS IN THE STARS: Solomon Kane #1	
		Robert E. Howard	$1.95
☐	11139	THE MICRONAUTS Gordon Williams	$1.95
☐	11276	THE GOLDEN SWORD Janet Morris	$1.95
☐	11418	LOGAN'S WORLD William Nolan	$1.75
☐	11835	DRAGONSINGER Anne McCaffrey	$1.95
☐	12044	DRAGONSONG Anne McCaffrey	$1.95
☐	10879	JONAH KIT Ian Watson	$1.50
☐	12019	KULL Robert E. Howard	$1.95
☐	10779	MAN PLUS Frederik Pohl	$1.95
☐	12269	TIME STORM Gordon R. Dickson	$2.25

Buy them at your local bookstore or use this handy coupon for ordering: